I0726869

Praise for **SSAFY**

"As a yoga teacher for over ten years, SSAFY has given me all the tools to help me guide my students through the world of technology. Now I know exactly what to do when my students want to take selfies or watch Hulu in class. I got rid of breathing and Savasana in all of my classes so my students can spend more time working on their abs. Thank you SSAFY!" — **@NIYAMAPAJAMAYOGI**

"Eddie, Roge, Carly and Asia are the best yoga teachers in the entire yoga community. They have way more followers than any other yogi, they are sexy AF, they know exactly which filters are getting the most likes on IG and they make me feel sexy and spiritual AF. Eddie's book and the entire SSAFY community have saved my life." — **@HOTASSYOGINISUPERSTAR**

"If you've always wanted to try yoga but you hated the idea that you had to put your phone away, then SSAFY is for you! Thanks to SSAFY, I still get to watch all of my favorite shows while I practice yoga. I do yoga in the shower, in the park, and I only wear bikinis when I practice yoga. Thank you, Eddie for your super spiritual book."
— **@SUNRISEBIKINIYOGA**

"Thank you Eddie for having the courage to write such a personal story and share your SSAFY journey with the entire world. Now, more people are going to wear less clothing, take more selfies and feel sexy and spiritual as fuck!"
— **@HIPHOPYOGASUPERSTAR**

"Before SSAFY, I took stupid meditation classes and restorative classes and wasted years of my life focused on the breath. Now, I never have to breathe again and I haven't taken a child's pose in over a year. Thank you SSAFY! You're the best!"
— **@CHILDSPOSEISFORLOSERS**

"SSAFY has made my Instagram explode, my abs are super sexy and now I feel so much more spiritual. Thank you SSAFY!" — **@SUPERSEXYWATERFALLYOGINI**

"I always wanted a yoga butt. Thank you SSAFY for making my booty look and feel sexy AF! I love my ass and SSAFY!" — **@BELFIEYOGAQUEEN**

If your yoga teacher doesn't make you feel sexy,
then it's time to find a new yoga teacher.

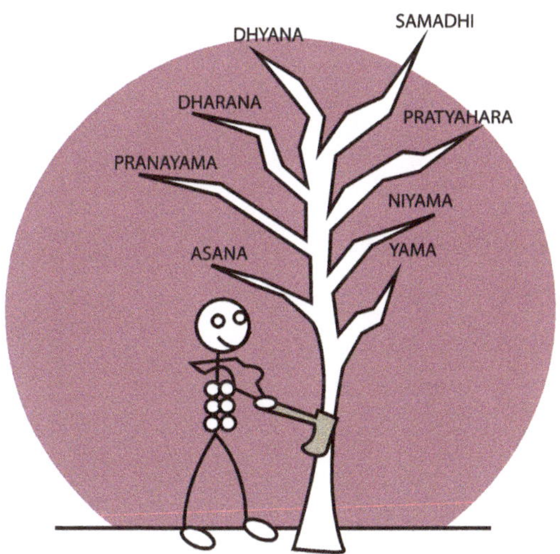

SSAFY

sexy spiritual AF yoga

What is SSAFY and What You Can Do to
Feel Sexy and Spiritual AF in Your Yoga Practice

Eddie Cohn

(Sexy and Spiritual AF)

Fore

Library of Canada Cataloguing in Publication data is available.

ISBN 9978-1-989528-12-9 (paperback edition)

ISBN 978-1-989528-13-6 (hardcover edition)

ISBN 978-1-989528-14-3 (e-book edition)

First Edition Printing 2021

Book and cover design by Clint Hutzulak

Imagery by Kristen Meyers

Edited by Sofia Capel

Inside author photo by Nathaniel Perales. Back cover photo by Sienna Farall.

Published in Canada by Storrar & Co., New Glasgow, NS.

For more information contact: publishing@storrar.co

Special discounts are available on quantity purchases by corporations, associations, and others. For details, contact the publisher at the address above.

For more information on the book and author please visit www.iameddiecohn.com or follow @eddiecohn

CONTENTS

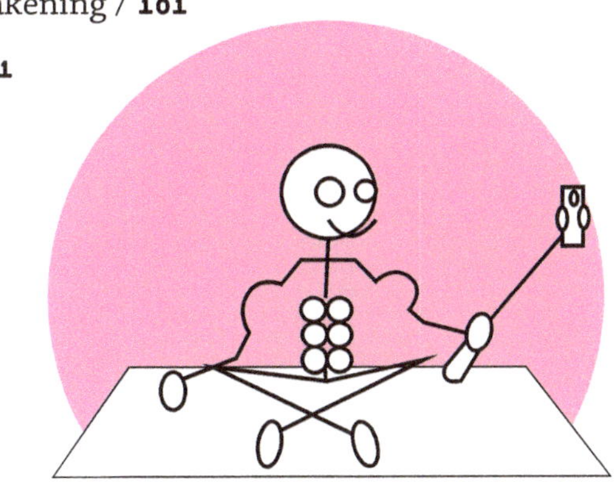

FOREWORD

I see your eyes wandering. Phone. TV. You're kind of reading, right? Distracted? Excellent. That's sexy AF. Is that Amazon Prime? Hulu? My bad. Netflix. *Emily in Paris*. So good. I binge-watched it last week while I held Handstand. Felt so spiritual. Okay. Keep watching Netflix while you read. I pretty much do everything while I watch Netflix. Eat, sleep, sex. I teach most of my Smoothie Yoga classes taking selfies and watching Netflix. My students love it. So spiritual. Have you ever drunk a smoothie while holding Warrior Two? You will. Oh, where's your iPad? How about your cell phone? They should be close by. Click, click, click. Snap, snap, snap. We have to take our first selfie together. Are you holding your phone in one hand and holding my book in the other? That would be the most spiritual for sure. Maybe a book reading selfie? Spiritual AF. Your followers will love that.

Let's try a selfie. I'm taking one. My tenth of the day. I wrote my entire book taking selfies. Totally spiritual. My yoga ass selfies look amazing in portrait mode. I use the vivid warm filter. Super sexy and spiritual. I know. Time for an ab selfie. If you've never taken one, you'll be an ab selfie maestro by the end of this book.

Full disclosure. Before SSAFY, I was a yoga joke. The laughing stock of yoga. I had a measly 92 followers on Instagram. I never thought about selfies. No stories. Clueless about filters and DMs. I couldn't hold Handstand or Scorpion Pose. I took way too many Savasanas. My abs were a flabby mess. I wore ugly yoga clothes. I was a gigantic big-time yoga loser with a Capital L. The George Costanza of yoga.

Post SSAFY? Now I'm freaking spiritual and sexy AF all the time. I have spiritual yoga highs that last for months without stopping. Did I mention I have 2 million followers thanks to SSAFY? Hang on. Correction: 2,080,000. Just peeped again. Eighty thousand new followers in the last three minutes. I take Handstands #everydamnday. I'm the proud owner of a sexy six-pack. I rarely wear much clothing, and when I do, it's usually little Speedos and tank tops. I don't sit cross-legged, I haven't taken a conscious breath in over a year, and I never take Child's Pose either. *Tell them about your new bathing suit sponsor. Instagram time! No, Eddie. Take a selfie. Tell them about your new sponsor!*

Okay. Yep. I have a new yoga thong sponsor. This thong retailer saw my butt cheeks on IG, and now they mail me these Euro thong-style handwoven bathing suits designed specifically for my ass. They're super spiritual, and my followers love them. I post side-angle ass selfies #everydamnday. I should probably take another one. Nah, maybe I'll make an organic green juice, take a Handstand in my kitchen and then take a selfie. An organic green juice Handstand selfie. You should try it. Wait. I know. SSAFY has a sick Handstand workshop this weekend. Why don't you take the workshop, take my Smoothie Standing Posture class afterward, hit up the ten-minute sweaty ab class with Roge, and then we'll work on some Smoothie Handstands. Now that's spiritual! K. Are you ready to join the SSAFY family and become sexy and spiritual AF? You're going to freaking love it. Your abs are going to look hot AF, and your IG is going to be on fire. 🔥🔥

ONE

clueless about ssafy

I got a little ahead of myself. I get excited when I introduce SSAFY to new students like you. Let's rewind because way before the sexual and spiritual euphoria of SSAFY, I was nowhere close to SSAFY material. Totally clueless about spirituality. Thirty-five years old, and I was anxious AF. Panic attacks. Ulcers. Barely could sleep. No girlfriend, and I bit my nails. I know. Gross. I started biting them when I was four. I'd put ketchup and sugar on them and bite them. My mom would catch me from across the room. 'Eddie. Stop biting your nails. Your hands are dirty. You're going to get a nail stuck in your lungs. I read about it in *Reader's Digest*. Nail particles get caught in your lungs, you can't breathe, and you'll die.'

Anxiety was probably in my DNA. My dad was anxious. My mom and brother were both anxious. It didn't help that there was no religion in our house either. *Hold up, dummy! You think religious people don't get anxious? Well maybe if I were religious, I wouldn't be so anxious. YOU are the reason why you're anxious. Not your mom. Not your dad. Not religion. Just* YOU! *Biting your nails like a big wuss.*

There are those voices. For most of my life, the negative voices bounced around inside my head. Back and forth. Telling me what to do. What not to do. What's wrong or what could go wrong. On a plane. *Plane crash.* Pain in my neck? *Neck cancer.* Back pain. *Back cancer.* Grand Canyon? *Don't trip and fall over the edge.* On a hike? *Bear attack.*

I was a complete germaphobe too, and to top it off, I was diagnosed with Rheumatoid Arthritis when I was twelve. RA is an auto-immune disease where the good cells inside your body get confused and attack your own body. Crohn's, RA, Lupus – these are all auto-immune conditions. For almost ten years, I was pretty much in and out of the hospital, popping pills, feeling like hell, and when the RA finally went away, that's when the panic attacks started to kick in. I felt hopeless and didn't know what else to do until one day, my fifth and final therapist had an idea...

CHAPTER 2

My First class
at the yoga sanctuary

The session started just like all of my hundreds of previous sessions…

"How are you feeling, Eddie?"

"I'm still not sleeping. Heartburn. I can't relax. I don't think the therapy is working. I keep coming here and it's the same pattern."

"You're being too hard on yourself."

"I still bite my nails. I had two panic attacks this week and my dentist told me I grind my teeth and I have to wear a night-guard."

"Maybe it's time we consider some pharmaceutical options."

"More pills?"

"There are some wonderful treatments available."

"What about the Xanax?"

"The Xanax is really just a temporary fix. These new medications should help you feel more relaxed."

"Isn't there anything else?"

"Well, have you thought of meditation or practicing yoga?"

"I can't even touch my toes."

"Yoga isn't about touching your toes."

"I don't know."

"In the right hands, it's a magical practice. It has a rich history, there are breathing techniques to help you relax, and I know the perfect studio. I think this could be life-changing. Socially and mentally, it could be a perfect fit."

"You really think so?"

"The Yoga Sanctuary of Spiritual Bliss. The teachers were trained in India. They have sound baths, full moon events, and there's Kirtan. You should consider it, Eddie. You could use a good sound bath."

After my session, I drove home, and for hours, I read articles about the so-called benefits of yoga. There were hundreds of postures with stories detailing the remedial and mysterious powers of yoga. It seemed too good to be true, but with a new attitude, the next day, I took my doctor's advice and drove to the Yoga Sanctuary of Spiritual Bliss. As I approached the studio, I could hear a group of athletic-looking people talking enthusiastically about yoga highs, third eyes, and their "blissful Savasana." Just like clockwork, the judgmental, negative voices started to pick up steam. *Listen to them. They sound like wackos. What the heck is a third eye? You're going to hate this place, dude. It's a cult. Waste of time. Stick with Xanax. Shut up! I am listening to Dr. Rob and trying this Sanctuary place. This has to work.*

Maybe it was the waterfall gently cascading in the lobby or the smell of sage incense, but when I walked through the front door, I immediately felt some tension in my shoulders release. As I approached the front desk, a young woman with soft brown eyes and wavy brown hair greeted me with a welcoming smile. She grabbed my hands and rubbed lavender oil in my palms.

"Namaste, yogi. My name is Ashwala."

"Hi, Ashwala. My doctor told me I should try yoga, and he said something about taking a bath?"

"You mean a sound bath. Yes, of course. We have one scheduled for tomorrow evening."

Ashwala kept massaging my palms and looked deeply into my eyes. *Why is she looking at me like that? Did she wash her hands?! She can't just massage people without washing her hands, can she? Eddie, would you be quiet and enjoy the healing hand massage. She isn't blinking. She won't stop staring at me. Why isn't she blinking?*

"Vishypu's class begins in a few minutes. He is our senior teacher. He just returned from India, and he specializes in hand chakras. What is your name, yogi?"

"Eddie."

"Welcome, Eddie. Have you ever had your chakras cleansed?"

"Not sure. I showered an hour ago."

"No, an internal chakra cleansing. I can feel an energy blockage in your hands."

I knew it. I have a blockage. I'm going to have a heart attack. A chakra heart attack. What the heck is a chakra? Did she say Chaka? Like Chaka Khan? Do I have a tumor? A chaka tumor? I have cancer. She can feel cancer in my hands. I have hand-chaka cancer!

"Should I see a doctor?"

"Vishypu will help you. You need a chakra cleansing."

"You sure I'm okay? I don't have cancer?"

"You need to breathe and connect with the yogi inside of you. Make yourself at home. Have some green tea. Vishypu's class begins very soon. I'll see you in there."

Ashwala brought her hands to her heart and bowed her head.

"May the light in me shine even brighter in you. I'll tell Vishypu it is your first time. I'll change clothes. Save me a spot."

Soft Indian chant music was playing, and everyone was either lying on their backs or peacefully sitting still with their legs crossed and eyes closed. A few students were lying down with one hand on their belly and one hand covering their heart. I found a spot towards the back of the room, put my mat down, and as I looked around, I was hopeful that one day I could feel a sense of calm like all the other yogis in class.

Wearing a floral top and matching floral leggings, Ashwala entered the studio, unrolled her mat and sat down next to me.

"You're going to love our studio. The energy of the teachers. The students. We pride ourselves on building a strong community." *She means cult. Get out of here, Eddie! It's a cult!*

"Vishypu is a true healer."

"I can't wait for him to clean my chakas." *Not chakas, Eddie!* CHAKRAS!"

Ashwala just smiled and turned to face the front of the room. She closed her eyes and crossed her legs while a few other yogis walked into class. The door gently closed as the lights dimmed. I turned around, and there stood the man, the myth, and the yoga legend himself, Vishypu. *Cult leader! He's going to seduce you into joining his cult. Get out of here, Eddie. Run!*

Vishypu had a proud and confident swagger when he walked around the room. He greeted each student with a hug and a warm

"Namaste." He was this angelic and soothing combination of Brad Pitt and Buddha. Tall. Handsome. He wore black puffy yoga pants and a tight white tank top. Earrings in both ears, mala beads around his neck, and bracelets up and down his forearm.

Vishypu eventually made his way towards Ashwala, embraced her with a hug and a gentle kiss on the cheek, and then turned towards me. Our eyes locked. He wasn't blinking either. *Smile at Vishypu! Say hello! Get out of here! Run! Smile!*

"And you must be Eddie."

"Nice to meet you, Vishypu."

"Ashwala says it's your first class."

"Kind of. I took a few YouTube classes last night but not sure I felt anything." *YouTube isn't yoga, you moron!*

"That's because you weren't connecting with the power of your breath. It always begins with the breath. Your breath is the force that connects you to the energy of the yogic earth inside the womb below the breath." *What the fuck did he just say?!*

Vishypu put his hands on my shoulders and motioned for me to stand up. He leaned in and gave me a hug. We stood there locked in each other's arms.

"Inhale with me, Eddie. Let's breathe together."

He took a gigantic inhale through his nose, and as he held me in his arms, like a tsunami, he sighed his breath all over me. *Yuck! He sprayed his germs all over the back of my neck! I need a shower. Where's the Purell? He better not have a cold. It's a cleansing breath! He has garlic breath! His germs are everywhere!*

"AHHHHHHHHHHHHH. Excellent yogi."

"Wow. I've never breathed like that."

"The breath is with you whenever you want to feel that connection to the loving kindness of your internal spirit. *There he goes again! Go! Leave this nuthouse. There's no such thing as an internal spirit.*

"Ashwala tells me your hand chakras are misaligned."

"Yeah, I probably should see a doctor."

"Nonsense. Welcome to class. If you get lost, Ashwala will help you along your yoga journey. Any injuries I should be aware of?"

"Well, my back is kind of…"

"Excellent. Let's get started."

Vishypu sat down at the front of the class, crossed his legs, and brought his hands to his heart. The entire roomful of yogis joined him in Sukhasana. A few minutes passed, and not a single movement, sound, or peep out of anyone. *Man, this is boring. Bunch of weirdos. How long are we going to sit here? You're supposed to breathe! Close your eyes and relax. Hello? Vishypu? When is the yoga going to start? This is yoga! When? NOW! This is yoga! My lower back is starting to hurt. Listen to Vishypu and breathe!*

Vishypu opened his mouth and belted out a deafening OMMMMMM. Ashwala and the rest of the class joined in. The walls and floor shook around me. My entire body vibrated. Ten, twenty, thirty, sixty seconds went by, and everyone was still OMMMMMMMMMMING away. *It's too loud in here. What are they doing!? They're saying Om! You always start class with an Om. How long are they going to say Om? Eddie! Shut up and Om. You should be Omming!*

As the Oms faded out, Vishypu opened his eyes. "Yogis, let's start in Child's Pose. Ground your body down. Notice the tickle of air below the nostrils. Notice that tickle tickle of air. Notice it. Keep noticing." *I am noticing! How long do I have to notice for!? Eddie, shut up and notice! Breathe! Notice your breath!*

"Notice the Mother Earth supporting your body and your breath. Notice yourself noticing. How do you feel when you notice? Where is your awareness as you notice what you're noticing within the breath? Breathe the earth that mothers your breath and be one with the holiness that is your breath." *He makes no sense! He's Looney Toons. What the heck did he just say? I can't take this place. I'm getting out of here. Would you sit down and notice your breath!*

For the next seventy-five minutes, we played a game of yoga *Simon Says*. When Vishypu instructed us to take Down Dog, the room took Down Dog. If he said Child's Pose, everyone put their head and hips down and took Child's Pose. He was our yoga lieutenant as we behaved like yoga soldiers following his commands. We moved from one posture to the next, always being reminded to return to the breath or to take Child's Pose.

We went through Up Dog, Down Dog, and all the Warrior postures. Backbends and Forward Folds. The A and B series. I was clueless, flailing my body from one posture to the next. I lost my balance and fell over a few times, but Ashwala quickly walked onto my mat, put her hands on my shoulders, and reassured me I was doing great.

We continued to move and breathe, and as class went on, I felt some slight tension in my shoulders release and let go. It was as though a door that had been slammed shut for years was opening up for the first time. The more I moved, breathed, and listened to Vishypu's instructions, my body and mind felt lighter, and I slowly relaxed. No Xanax or alcohol. No therapy. No crying. Just yoga. Through the simple movement of my body and the inhale and exhale of my breath, I felt a sense of freedom I had never experienced.

Vishypu came up from behind me in Warrior Two and placed his hands on my shoulders.

"Eddie, feel the breath in each inhale and exhale. I can see your chakras trying to realign. Relax the shoulders and the jaw. Virabhadrasana Two, everyone! And continue to breathe! Never let go of the breath!"

With my eyes closed, I held Warrior Two. Taking monstrous inhales and exhales, I suddenly felt something soft and round being placed around my neck. *He's putting anal beads on your neck! He's a perv! You're wearing anal beads! Get out of here, Eddie! They're healing mala beads you idiot!* I opened my eyes and saw Vishypu standing directly in front of me, placing his wooden mala beads around my neck.

"I dedicate these beads to your breath and your hand chakras. Let me hear you breathe."

I took an inhale through my mouth.

"Through the nose, Eddie. Deeper. Again."

I took another inhale.

"Deeper. Take a deep cleansing breath." *Does he not see me breathing?!*

I breathed again.

"Even deeper. I want to feel your breath permeate through each cell." *Can he not see that I am breathing!? I am breathing! Would you listen to Vishypu and breathe deeper!? How deep do I have to breathe?! Deeper! And thank him for the mala beads!*

"Vishypu, I can't take your mala beads."

"They're a gift. They will remind you that the yoga is always inside of you, and the breath is your guide." *What am I supposed to do with these things? You wear them, you idiot! YOU JUST GOT SOME HEALING MALA BEADS! His sweat is all over them. They smell. These beads are gross. EDDIE! They're anti-anxiety beads. You'll never have another panic attack as long as you wear his beads!*

Vishypu walked towards the front of class. "Make your way to Child's Pose, yogi bears. Send me your breath, and I'll send you my breath so we can breathe together as one loving breath."

The entire room took another deep inhale and let out one final exhale. With my head down and my eyes closed, I could sense my body gently let go as the swirling thoughts inside my head began to slow down. Vishypu dimmed the lights and led us to final resting Savasana.

"Notice the breath when you breathe and how you keep noticing what you notice is happening when you breathe and notice. Soak in Mother Earth's loving breath from her womb of the soulful leaves of grass."

What does that even mean?! You should breathe like grass! How the heck do I breathe like grass? I had no idea what Vishypu was talking about, but it didn't matter. With Vishypu's beads around my neck, I could feel a transformation happening inside of my body. I lay in final resting Savasana when after a few moments, I felt Vishypu place his hands on my body. His face was no more than a few inches away from me. *He's going to kiss me! It's a sex cult! HELP! Relax! He's trying to transfer his healing energy to you. He's breathing all over me! I'm definitely catching a cold.*

He pressed his hands down on my shoulders. *He's going to strangle me. HELP! He wants to kill me! He's giving you a neck massage! He's trying to help you relax!*

"Allow your body and mind to let go. The thoughts are distractions to your soul. Allow the Brahman and the strength of your spirit to relinquish the hold of the yamas and niyamas." *What the fuck is a yama?! Would you speak English?! I have no idea what you're talking about.*

"Reeeeeeeelaaaaaxxxxxxxxxx."

Vishypu pressed my shoulders firmly into my mat. He rubbed my neck, placed his hands over my heart, and whispered into my ear, "Shanti, yogi. May the breath always be with you."

Vishypu was like a Yogi Obi-Wan Kenobi, and as I lay in final Savasana, my body and mind started to let go. I felt the softness of each cell and muscle in my body. I felt cells I had never felt before. Wrist and buttocks cells. Arm cells and nose cells. Forehead cells. Elbow cells. As the roomful of yogis rose to a seated position, Vishypu sat at the front of the class and brought his hands to his heart and bowed his head.

"May the presence of peace and beauty in you make the world more peaceful and beautiful. Namaste, yogis."

Ashwala reached over and took my hands.

"Eddie, I don't even recognize you! How are your chakras? Let me feel them."

"I'm not sure. You think they're fixed?"

Ashwala kept massaging my hands. "I have never felt such perfectly aligned chakras. Much more balanced. And I see this golden-yellow hue hovering over you."

"You do? Where?" I looked up and around me but saw nothing.

"You can't see it, but I do."

As I rolled up my mat, students congratulated me on finishing my first class with Vishypu and welcomed me to the studio. I was even invited to an evening meditation circle when Ashwala put her arms around me and gave me one last hug. "Welcome to our community."

"Ashwala, I feel like I'm high."

"It's the natural euphoric energy created by the stillness of your breath, the movement of your body combined with Vishypu's energy. Your parasympathetic nervous system is showering you with Gaba. It creates a yoga high."

"Feels like I'm drunk."

"It's the Gaba exploding inside of you. Try listening to some calm music when you get home or drink some green tea to sustain your Gaba levels."

For the next few hours, my body felt like a puffy white cloud floating in the sky. I was the perfect blend of calmness and contentment. Whether taking a shower, feeding my cats, or watching TV, I felt the euphoric power of a yoga high. No sudden urge to bite my nails, pop a pill or drink a glass of wine. As I lay on my couch, I held Vishypu's beads tightly in my hands and imagined living a life just like Vishypu where I could sit still, slow down and calmly breathe.

In bed, I fantasized about how I'd never have to go to therapy or live another day feeling intense levels of anxiety. I kept thanking Vishypu inside of my head. For the mala beads. For teaching me how to finally breathe and for giving me the chance to experience my first ever Gaba yoga high. I wished Ashwala and Vishypu one more Namaste, and as I fell asleep, holding Vishypu's mala beads, I was convinced I would never feel anxious again.

CHAPTER 3
NOT A VERY SEXY PANIC ATTACK

4:30 AM. MEOW! MEOW! MEOW! My cat Nellie woke me up pretty much every morning, but today I was more annoyed than usual. She was disrupting my yoga high. Meow! She walked right up to my face. MEOW. MEOW. *Nellie! Down! Go back to bed. You're ruining my yoga high. I'm going to get sick. My immune system needs eight hours of sleep! Relax, Eddie. Breathe. Touch Vishypu's beads. Vishypu is with you. Breathe, little yogi.*

Meow-meow-meow.

No, Nellie! Down! *Relax and touch the beads, Eddie. Listen to Vishypu. Trust the yoga. Close your eyes and breathe.*

I shoved Nellie off my bed. I thought of Vishypu as I massaged the mala beads. *Look at you. Pathetic. Touching round wooden anal balls in your hands while you think of some weirdo named Vishypu. These are meditation beads! Anal beads! Meditation! Anal! Shut up!*

CRASH BOOM BAM BAM BAM!!

It was trash day. Metal garbage cans were bouncing and clanking in the alley. *It's over. My yoga high is definitely gone. No more Gaba. Just breathe, Eddie. You must listen for the sound of your breath. I can't hear anything! Feel the Gaba. I don't feel any Gaba!*

Nellie hopped back on my bed and let out another loud MEOW! A car alarm was blaring outside, and the neighbor's Rottweilers started to bark. As Nellie started to play a game of cat and mouse with my feet, my heart started to beat faster. *Vishypu, help! My heart. I'm sweating. I'm feeling anxious. I need a Xanax. Just breathe, Eddie. I'm trying! Just breathe. I AM! Keep breathing. Feel the Gaba. There is no more fucking Gaba! Breathe. I am breathing, but it's not working! Just breathe, Eddie. Shut up about the breathing! AHHHHHH!*

The anxiety was too powerful. Tension built up in my shoulders. My neck and head began to ache. My breath grew more rapid, and my heart wouldn't stop racing. A panic attack was just around the corner, and all I could think about was...

WHAT THE HECK HAPPENED TO MY YOGA HIGH!?!?!

It has to be the mala beads! They're broken! Maybe one of them fell off while I was sleeping? Nellie grabbed it! She thinks it's a toy. I bet one of them is scattered on the floor.

I lifted the sheets and then looked under the bed, but not a single bead anywhere. The walls started to cave in. Nellie wouldn't stop meowing. The dogs were still barking outside. My chest pounded even faster. I leaped out of bed. I couldn't take it. I needed a Xanax NOW. *No Xanax! It's five in the morning! I'm freaking out over here! My yoga high is gone! I can't breathe, and I have dysfunctional mala beads! There's no way these mala beads work for only ten hours. They have to be broken. Vishypu gave me fucked up beads. Go back to The Yoga Sanctuary and see Vishypu. Ask for some new beads!*

Vishypu was scheduled to teach the first class of the day at six. As I walked in, Ashwala was sitting behind the counter, lighting some candles and preparing for class.

"Ashwala!"

My chest felt like it was about to explode.

"Namaste, Eddie. You're back so soon. May the light in me guide you…"

"Yeah, yeah. The light in you is in me."

"How is your breath this morning? Are you here to sign up for our chakra workshop? Maybe a sound bath?"

"My yoga high, it's gone! I have to take another class. Where's Vishypu?"

Ashwala took hold of my hands.

"You have to breathe."

"Look at me. I'm breathing. It's not working."

"You must learn to trust your breath, and that takes time."

"My yoga high is completely gone. No more Gaba. It has to be the beads. I think they're broken."

"The beads work fine."

"I went to bed, felt high on life and relaxed, and then there were trash cans, dogs barking, my cat Nellie was jumping on me."

"Aww, you have a cat?"

"She took my yoga high away! I keep touching these mala beads, but nothing is working!"

"Eddie, why don't you stay for class? Calexico is teaching the six."

Calexico?! Who the fuck is Calexico?

"Where's Vishypu? The schedule says Vishypu is at six. I looked online. It clearly said Vishypu is teaching!"

"I'm sorry. Vishy has a sub. He is preparing for his sound bath this evening."

"But I drove here to see Vishypu."

"It must not have been updated in the system. Calexico is an excellent teacher. He would be happy to help you bring back your Gaba levels."

"But what about my beads? Can you at least call Vishypu?"

"I'm going to make you some tea. The tea should be very calming. Calexico will be here any minute. You can show him your beads."

I don't want to talk to Calexico! I am freaking out over here! Relax, Eddie. You're going to be fine. Calexico is probably an excellent teacher. I NEED TO SEE VISHYPU!! I can't breathe. I want some new beads!

I hadn't even taken a sip of my tea when Ashwala started talking again. "By the way, Eddie, I didn't get the chance to tell you about our memberships. We have this great monthly plan where —"

Does she not see I'm about to have a heart attack?! She is talking about memberships, and I'm about to die! My heart kept beating faster. The anxiety was back in full force. A panic attack was seconds away.

"— If you join today, your first month will be half off, and you'll have unlimited access to all of our workshops and sound baths...."

With no sign of Vishypu, I started to feel dizzy and fell to my knees.

"EDDIE! Are you okay?"

"Ashwala. Please. I need my yoga high back. Please call Vishypu. Yes, I'll join. You have to help me."

"Great! I'll sign you up for our premium monthly package, which gives you unlimited access to all full-moon and sound bath events."

I bent over and started to cry.

"Eddie, what's wrong? We should be celebrating as you begin your lifelong yoga journey at the Yoga Sanctuary." *I have to come here for the rest of my life!? DUH! It's a cult! You're stuck here forever. You're never leaving!*

"I have to talk to Vishypu. He has to look at my beads. My yoga high, I'm begging you. Call Vishypu."

Ashwala picked up the phone. I was still crying.

"Vishy. Sorry to interrupt your morning meditation. Eddie's crying and very upset. He was in class last night. He wants to talk to you. It's urgent."

Ashwala handed me the phone.

"Vishypu?"

"Eddie. Namaste. How may I help you?"

"Vishypu, is that you?"

"It's me, Eddie. How is your breath?"

"Terrible!"

"Take a deep inhale, Eddie."

"I think it's the mala beads. They're broken. I keep touching them. I'm still wearing them but I feel nothing."

"Eddie, you have to breathe."

"I keep breathing but it's not working. I think I need some new beads."

"There is nothing wrong with your mala beads. It takes time to trust your breath and grow within your practice. That's why they call it a practice. I have a sound bath this evening. You should come."

"Can you at least look at my beads? And make sure they're okay?"

"I'd be happy to tonight."

"Thank you, Mr. Vishy."

"Namaste."

"Namaste to you, too."

Still trembling, I handed the phone back to Ashwala.

"Are you feeling any better? Why don't you stay for Calexico's class."

"Okay. And sign me up for the sound bath."

"And the membership?"

"Yes. All of it. The sound bath. Calexico's class. Give me everything!"

Ashwala saw my distress and wrapped a yoga blanket around my shoulders, refilled my teacup, pulled out a contract, and helped me off the floor. She kept reassuring me everything would be okay. As Ashwala wiped tears from my eyes, she discreetly handed me a pen.

"You're going to be okay, Eddie."

"I just want my yoga high back."

"You'll have a Gaba high in no time. Just sign the contract."

"And this is just for a year?" *NO! Don't do it! You'll never leave!*

"Well, technically, yes, but I have a strong sense you'll be a member for many years. Here's the contract, Eddie. Sign it."

Don't do it! It's a scam! You don't need yoga! Yes, I do! No! Yes! You'll never leave!

The critical voices went back and forth inside of my head. Ashwala looked serenely into my eyes and once again said, "Sign the contract." I felt trapped, but deep down, I knew I had no choice. I was tired of the anxiety and the useless therapy sessions.

I was tired of feeling uncomfortable in my own skin, and Ashwala had this trance-like look in her eyes that was hypnotizing, so I signed up for the ultra-premium membership. Unlimited everything. Each class, sound bath, full moon event, and chakra cleanse were all included as I prepared to devote my life to Vishypu, Ashwala, and The Yoga Sanctuary of Spiritual Bliss.

"Perfect," Ashwala said after I signed the contract. "Let's go for a kombucha to celebrate!"

"A kuh-what?"

"A kombucha. I know this cute little place next door."

"What about Calexico's class?"

"You'll still make it. Let's go."

Cafe Thankful was an eclectic/all-organic cafe specializing in wheatgrass shots, almond butter shakes, and organic whole wheat and non-dairy pastries. A chalkboard outside revealed today's kombucha on tap: Pineapple Rose. A sycamore tree with long hanging limbs extended from the middle of a shaded outdoor dining area. Kirtan filled the air as yogis and yoginis sat around, quietly reading spiritual musings from yoga texts. A few others were journaling, sipping on their warm tea, or talking about their morning meditation.

I grabbed a menu as Ashwala led me to a cozy table outside.

"Everything here is organic. The kombucha and wheatgrass are amazing. They grow their own grass right in the backyard garden."

"Sounds yummy." *Barf. Did you look at the menu? There's no actual food here. Seeds, grass, and tea. What the heck is a wheatgrass shot? It's liquid dirt and grass. You're going to hurl everywhere.*

A waitress approached our table. Her hair was tied up in a ponytail by a rose stem. Star-shaped blue and red tattoos were sketched on the backs of her fingers.

"Hi, Jules. I'll take today's kombucha. And how fresh is the grass?"

"Super fresh. I pulled it this morning."

"K. One shot for each of us. Some chia seeds for the table. What else do you want, Eddie?"

"I'll have the… um… give me… uh… how about one organic blueberry scone and the kombuck drink thing."

Ashwala smiled. "Jules. Two of everything. We'll share."

"Would you like the scone sprinkled with sunflower seeds or pine nuts?"

Ashwala could tell I couldn't make up my mind.

"Sunflower seeds. And two lemons for the shots."

Ashwala told me more about the class offerings at the Sanctuary. Reiki, full moon events, weekly meditation, and healing zen circles on the first Friday of each month. She explained how she was from Irvine and moved to Santa Monica once world-renowned yoga master Vishypu opened up his first studio. As she spoke, I couldn't stop thinking about my mala beads and lowering Gaba levels.

"You sure my beads aren't broken? Where did my Gaba go?"

"The Gaba is still there. Vishy will help you reignite the Gaba. I promise."

"You make it sound so easy."

Ashwala smiled. "Eddie, you're in good hands. Vishy was taught directly by BKS Iyengar, and he's been practicing since the age of four. Three times a year, he goes on a month-long Vipassana to India. We're blessed he opened a studio here in the States."

Her kind words and soothing voice helped me relax. Ashwala had the most beautiful brown eyes that glimmered when she smiled.

"What about you?" I asked. "Do you teach?"

"No, not yet. Vishy has a two-month teacher training in Santorini this summer. I'm dying to go."

Ashwala went on to tell me about the value of a home practice. She mentioned some of the introductory yoga props on sale at the Sanctuary. Cushions and bolsters, straps, eye pillows, and foam blocks. Ashwala also told me where she buys her favorite lavender candles and offered to help me set up my own meditation den at home.

Ashwala asked, "You have a cat, right?"

"Two. Nellie and Leo."

"Yogis are such cat people. My cat always wants to sit on my lap when I meditate."

I noticed Ashwala's eyes glance towards the front door. Three men wearing bright fluorescent Speedos and tank tops walked inside, taking selfies. Ashwala immediately covered one side of her face with her hand and looked down at the table, pretending to study the menu. In a flash, one of the guys jumped up on a table and held Handstand. His friend was sprinkling powdered sugar on his abs and took a powdered sugar ab selfie while drinking a wheatgrass shot.

"Woah! Did you see that, Ashwala?! Look at what they're doing!"

Ashwala whispered, "Shh… please don't say my name. I don't want them to know I'm here."

As the two men continued to take Handstand and selfies, the leader of the pack, with a Steven Seagal swagger, peeped towards us and waltzed in our direction. His black hair was tied up in a bun, he had a toned body, tattoos, earrings, and he was wearing a skin-tight yellow wife-beater to match his tight-fitting Speedo.

"Ashwala?" the man said with his pelvis leaning slightly toward us. "I thought that was you! How the hell are ya?"

Ashwala stopped pretending to read the menu and glanced up. "Oh. Hi, Roge."

"Come on. Let's take a kombucha selfie. I'll tag you. Love the outfit. Who's your friend?"

"Hey, I'm Eddie!"

"How's it going, dude? He turned to Ashwala again. "You sure you don't want to be our new night manager? Asia just graduated from our ten-hour TT and starts teaching next week. We need someone to step in. You'd be perfect."

"That's okay, Roge. I'm good at the Sanctuary."

"Sanctuary, Shmankuary. You're not stuck doing that boring old yoga with Vishypu, are you? Dude, the man can't even hold a Handstand."

Ashwala covered my ears with her hands. "Don't listen to him, Eddie."

"What, I'm just saying it's a little weird that some supposed famous guru can't even hold a simple Handstand. Just a little peculiar."

The man holding Handstand howled to Roge. "Hey, Roge! Quick, take a story! My followers are going to flip over this Handstand. Put a smoothie on the table, and I'll try and take a sip."

"Love it, Skone! So spiritual!" Roge pulled out his phone and captured some pics, then turned back to face Ashwala.

"Ok, Ash. Just wanted to pop over. I'm launching a new season on my YouTube channel next week, combining yoga with the spiritual aura of adult entertainment. It's gonna be huge. You should come by. Filming starts next week. I'll send you a DM on the Gram."

"Roge, you know I'm not on Instagram."

"STILL?! One selfie with me, you'll be at like 10,000 followers. You'll feel so much more spiritual. Maybe pick up some sponsors."

"I don't need sponsors."

"You should bring your friend."

"Goodbye, Roge."

"See you, man!" I said as Roge winked at me and noticed my mala beads.

"Dig the beads, bro."

"Thanks!"

Ashwala raised her voice, "Roge, GOODBYE!"

Roge turned to re-join his crew. "Skone, let's go to the beach and practice our Surfboard Handstands! Gordo, let's peek at those powdered sugar ab selfies and pick a filter and post 'em."

And they were gone.

"Who are they?!" I asked with big eyes.

"Oh... just idiots. They don't take yoga seriously."

"That was yoga!? Can Vishypu teach me how to do that?"

"None of that is yoga. Ignore them. Now, where were we? When can I come over and meet your kitties?"

Over the next few months, I took class virtually #everydamnday at the Sanctuary. I studied the yin and restorative postures, and I went to weekly sound baths with Ashwala. I looked forward to my chakra cleansing each week, and I participated in my first meditation circle and Reiki session. My mala beads never left my side as I started each morning with a fifteen-minute meditation practice. I acquired a vast collection of incense and oils, and I even bought yoga props to develop my own home practice. My therapy sessions lessened, my nails grew back, and I stopped relying on Xanax to help me relax. While the critical voices never completely went away, the panic attacks lessened. I even thought about taking a teacher training with Vishypu. Life had never been so good, but it was about to get even better!

CHAPTER 4
TWO YOGA GODDESSES

It was just another evening yoga class like all the others I had taken at the Sanctuary. Ashwala and I were grabbing dinner afterwards at the new Almond Nut Cafe, and she was going to introduce me to her cat, Guava. I checked in at the front desk and found my usual unassuming spot in the corner towards the front row. I unrolled my mat, grabbed two wooden blocks, and hung out in Child's Pose while the rest of the yogis made their way into the studio. I heard a few more "Namastes" and a couple "Shantis." All the pre-class rituals you would expect at the Sanctuary; Savasana, Sukhasana, hugs, and whispering.

We were about five minutes into class. The teacher had us lying in Savasana when suddenly, the studio door burst open. The Sanctuary had a strict no-latecomer policy, but the interlopers didn't seem to care, as a loud roar echoed from the lobby. I peeked up from my Savasana and noticed two drop-dead gorgeous yoginis chatting, laughing, and smiling as they walked into class, waving glow sticks around. They were unlike any yogini I had ever seen at the Sanctuary. They both wore sunglasses. One of them was wearing a tiny red bikini, while the other wore low-cut, see-through yoga pants and the tiniest tank top. Bracelets dangled from their necks and arms, and they strutted into class on five-inch stilettos. But the craziest part was they were taking selfies as they walked into class.

A few students stood up and yelled out, "You can't take selfies in here!"

"Put your phone away!"

"No G-strings in class."

"The Yoga Sanctuary of Spiritual Bliss is A SACRED SPACE!"

A group of students stood up and threw yoga bolsters at them. I even heard a smattering of BOOs. A man behind me quickly grabbed his phone and snuck in a few photos. I later found out he worked for the Venice Beach Yoga Paparazzi and made over $2,000 a photo. Another guy pulled out pen and paper and begged for an autograph while another student asked if they'd take a selfie with him. The yelling and protests continued as a few other students started to hurl foam blocks in their direction.

The teacher finally clapped his hands and raised his voice, "Everyone. Put the bolsters down. Focus your energy on your own mat and make your way to Downward Facing Dog. Focus on your breathing."

"Would you tell those two strippers to get out of here!?" a student yelped.

"They aren't yogis!"

"This isn't a dance club! It's a yoga studio!"

The teacher responded, "Everyone, focus your attention on your own mat and breath. No judgment within these walls."

The room quieted down, but there was still a nervous, unsettled energy in the air like another yoga bolster fight could erupt at any second. *Just listen to the teacher, Eddie. Sure, those women are super hot but don't pay any attention to them. Dude. Are you nuts? Look at them! Their boobs are about to explode out of their shirts! Breathe and focus on Down Dog!*

I was in my Dog when all of a sudden… **SNAP**!! Two yoga mats smacked the floor on either side of me. I looked up and saw the same two yoga supermodels directly beside me. Up close, they were even sexier with perfectly sculpted bodies and their massive breasts pressing through their tank tops.

I tried to focus, but instead of taking Down Dog, the two yoga hotties next to me whipped out their phones, started taking selfies, and then… PLACED MINI TRIPODS AT THE TOP OF THEIR MATS. *What the hell are they doing!? They can't take video selfies in a yoga class, can they?*

They connected their video cameras, aligned them in "perfect selfie position" and started waving hello to their "IG family." Then all of a sudden, they magically just hopped right up into Handstand. Like two birds floating in the air, their bodies hung upside down while the rest of class was in Down Dog.

It was like Yoga Cirque du Soleil when without warning, they did the unimaginable; they simultaneously lifted one hand in the air and held One-Handed Handstand. With that, more yogis rolled up their mats and stomped out of the studio.

"They're ruining my yoga high!"

"They don't breathe! They don't take Savasana!"

"That isn't yoga! They should be banned!"

The outbursts slowly died down as the teacher guided us to our first Child's Pose. *What the heck are we doing in Child's Pose? I can't see anything! Listen to the teacher. Head down. This Child's Pose is needed. But I can't see what's going on next to me! I wanna try that Handstand thing! And who is this lame teacher obsessed with Child's Pose? This sub is terrible. I bet Vishypu would let me stare at these hotties. Vishypu would never allow them into class. They're hijacking the Sanctuary!*

With the room settled, the teacher released us from Child's Pose and led us into Warrior Two. I bent my front thigh deep to a ninety-degree angle, reached my arms wide, closed my eyes, and tried to focus on my yoga. *Open your eyes! Don't do it. Your Warrior Two looks great. Focus on your breathing! Open your eyes! No, Eddie. No peeking. Open your eyes!* NOW!

I open my eyes, and the two mystery yoginis are now taking selfies WHILE HOLDING Warrior Two! ON THE SAME YOGA MAT! A foam block flew across the room and nearly hit me in the face. A student yelled out from the back of class, "None of that is yoga! Get them out of here!"

Their arms extended out in perfect selfie position as they pressed their half-naked and sweat-drenched bodies up against one another. The two guys behind me dropped to their knees and started shooting videos. More groans, hissing, and yelling echoed in class.

The teacher could sense he was losing the attention of his students. He reminded us to "focus on our own mat. Allow the breath to energize your yogic energy." I closed my eyes again and did my best to ignore the yoga strip show and the yogic energy inside my shorts. When I opened my eyes, the two sexy yoginis were back on their own mats. One of them was looking directly at me. *Say hello! Wave! You don't wave in yoga! Take a selfie! No selfies in yoga! Maybe she wants to do yoga with me on my mat? Would you stop it?!*

I glanced in her direction and quietly said, "Hello."

She responded, "Your Warrior Two looks super hot. You have to take a selfie." She had this soft sultry voice when she spoke.

"A what?" I asked. *Would you stop talking and go back to your yoga!*

"A selfie!"

"Really. I'm okay. Thank you." *You are such a loser. Take the selfie!*

"Come on! You look super spiritual." She held out her selfie stick. *Don't you dare grab that selfie stick! Who does she think she is, interrupting your practice?*

"I'm just going to breathe." *Yuck. You sound pathetic. Breathe like a sissy little girl.*

She wouldn't let up. "No one cares about breathing. Come on. Your followers will love it."

Suddenly, my Warrior Two Princess proceeded to WALK ONTO MY MAT, came up from behind me, and pressed her hips directly against my buttocks. She grabbed my arms and lifted them in the air, and said, "What's the point of yoga without posting it?"

She pressed my front thigh to ninety degrees as we created this erotic version of Double Warrior Two. I felt her hair touch my shoulders. Her sweat mixed with mine. She leaned in and whispered, "Doesn't that feel so spiritual?" *Look at me! Look how spiritual I look! You two are disgusting. And that isn't yoga! Oh, come on! This is yoga! That's definitely not yoga! This is the best freaking yoga pose I have ever taken.*

She raised her phone high in the air as we continued the sexual exploration of Selfie Warrior Two Pose with me as her sexual spiritual partner. One selfie after another. Click-click-click like some selfie maestro as she continued to press her shimmering body against mine. She whispered, "These selfies are going to get us so many followers." *Followers? Hello! Wake up, you idiot! She's going to post these! Where?! On Instagram! What the heck do you think she's doing?*

My body was shivering from the spiritual euphoria of Double Warrior Two. We pressed our hips into each other when suddenly, a huge round yoga bolster flew across the room and hit me on the top of my head.

"YOU TWO ARE GROSS!" A voice shrieked from across the room.

My sexy selfie yoga partner didn't seem phased at all. "Ignore them. They're just jealous. You're doing great. I'm Asia, and that's Carly. I'll tag you. What's your IG?"

"My what?"

"Your Insta?"

"Instacart?"

Asia smiled. "Instagram, silly!"

Asia posted a few stories and a selfie, strolled back onto her mat, and flew into another Handstand.

YOU ARE AN IDIOT! INSTAGRAM! INSTA MEANS INSTAGRAM! Not Instacart, you loser! You just ruined it! She posted that pic and didn't even tag you! Wait! I'm Eddie Cohn! @eddiecohn! Too late, loser. Would you stop crying and listen to the teacher who is trying to get your attention! Teacher? What teacher? The teacher! At the front of class!

I had been so engrossed with my yoga Ménage à Trois, I completely forgot I was in a yoga class. I looked around and noticed most of the women had already stormed out of class without a single Namaste. The only students left were the men who weren't even holding any postures. They just sat on their mat, gawking with their mouths wide open.

The teacher finally broke the collective trance, clapped his hands, and guided the room to the more dynamic flow part of class. The B Series. Chair, Updog, Downdog, Plank, and Warrior One. I was in the midst of my flow when I began to feel a shift of energy swirl around inside my body. My skin tingled, and after a few rounds of B, my body was burning up. My shirt was drenched with sweat. Before I knew it, I had this uncontrollable urge to rip my shirt off.

Take it off, Eddie. The voices inside my head wouldn't stop. *Take it off, you stud! Show Asia your hot bod.* HA. *You mean, wimpy bod. You're a stud, Eddie. Take it off.* I reached down, grabbed my shirt, yanked it over my head, and flung it to the floor. I raised my arms up in the air like Andy Dufresne from *The Shawshank Redemption.* I felt free from the tight annoying grip of my unsexy shirt. Asia and Carly raised their arms high in the air and screamed, "Go, sexy yogi, Go!" With my shirt off and the two sexy yoga goddesses by my side, I turned the rest of my B into the greatest yoga flow of my life.

We reached the end of class and made our way to final resting Savasana. I lay down and prepared myself for Corpse Pose when I heard someone rolling up their mat. I took a peek and saw Asia. She was skipping Savasana.

"Asia, what about Savasana?"

"Nah. I have to post these selfies and take some shower pics. By the way, the selfie we took already has 16,000 likes. We look super-spiritual. I'll post the rest and tag you. What's your handle?"

"My handle?"

"Your Instagram name."

"Oh yeah, @eddiecohn."

"K, I'll tag you." Asia opened up Instagram and immediately looked repulsed.

"Eww."

"What's wrong?"

"You only have ninety-two followers?! Yikes. That's not very spiritual."

LOSER EDDIE strikes again! You're done. Asia definitely isn't going to tag you.

"It's okay," she said. "This should help. We'll work on your Instagram and get it looking more spiritual. K. Follow me and come take class with me. I'll DM you."

And like that, Asia was gone. *Wait! What class!? Come back! I wanna take more selfies!*

Carly wasn't in Savasana either. She was posting a Live Instagram feed while holding a Forward Fold. She was telling her followers about the hair products and moisturizers she likes to use after class. As for me and my boring Savasana, I couldn't stop fidgeting. *Would the teacher please say Namaste already? What is taking him so long? Namaste! Say Namaste!*

The teacher finally brought his hands to his heart and ended class with a "NAMASTE." *About freaking time! Time to get out of here and find Asia on IG!* I grabbed my towel and was about to put my shirt back on when Carly grabbed my arm. "Stop! What are you doing?"

"What's wrong?"

"Keep the shirt off. It's time for a sweaty post-class selfie. Get your phone. I'll show you."

"My phone's in the car."

"Ugh. K, Rule #1. Never leave your phone in the car."

Carly handed me her phone and selfie stick.

"Just use mine."

I took her phone and selfie stick. *What the heck do I do with this thing? You take a selfie, you moron! But I don't take selfies. What the hell is a sweaty selfie? Should I put my shirt back on? What did she just say?! Keep the shirt off!*

Carly stood there, staring at me as I stalled. *Do an ass selfie, dude. Totally hot! I am not taking a selfie of my ass. Well, don't just stand there. She's waiting!*

I settled for a bicep selfie. I flexed my arm and smiled at the camera. Snap. Perfect. Done. Easy enough. I handed the phone back to Carly.

"How's that?"

Pathetic. Totally awful.

"That was terrible!"

Told you.

"Did you even add a filter?"

"A filter of what?"

"Stop it. You have to take my class. What's your name?"

Does she want my real name or my Instagram name? INSTAGRAM! Tell her Instagram!

"@eddiecohn."

Carly smiled. "Okay. At Eddie Cohn. Nice to meet you, at Eddie Cohn."

Carly grabbed me around the shoulder, leaned in, and pressed her slick body up against mine. She aligned her phone in "optimal sweaty selfie position," and she was off. Snapping away like some sort of selfie wizard. Snap-snap-snap.

"I'm totally storying all of these."

"On Instagram?"

"DUH! YES! Instagram, TikTok, and my YouTube. You're going to feel so much more spiritual. K, just posted it. I'm Carly, by the way."

"Thanks, Carly."

"Just tagged you. Hopefully, that'll give it a little kick. You should come take my class at SSAFY." Carly gazed at me from head to toe. "I see some serious SSAFY potential in you. I'll DM you the address."

Carly ran out of the studio capturing stories and signing more autographs, while the worst yoga teacher of all time walked around the room, with his hands at his heart, wishing us a final Namaste. *Barf. Enough with the Namastes, loser! Get your phone! Get out of here! Ask Carly for an autograph! Go-Eddie-Go!*

I grabbed my mat and hustled out of there as fast as I could. In the lobby, it was like a post-Academy Awards yoga party. Students screaming, waving, begging for selfies and autographs while the yoga paparazzi waited outside, hoping to catch a glimpse of Carly's spiritual outfit. Asia pulled up to the curb in a red convertible and slammed on the brakes. Carly sprinted outside and, in one smooth motion, hopped into Car Handstand, and just like that, the two sex yoga goddesses were gone.

Feeling feverish, my body still shook from the intensity of Selfie Warrior Two and the threesome yoga party. There was a tingling sensation throughout my body, and while I didn't know it at the time, I was experiencing my first SSAF yoga high.

As I buried my face in my towel, I wondered if I would ever practice with Carly or Asia again? *Hello! Phone! Would I ever feel this high without Carly and Asia by my side? Your phone! What are you doing? You need to find Carly on Instagram!* Would they want to take another Warrior Two Selfie? *Earth to yoga dumb-dumb. Get off your ass and get back to your phone! Follow them! SSAFY! HELLO! Sexy Yoga!*

I grabbed my yoga mat and was almost out the door when I heard Ashwala call out my name.

"Eddie, wait for me. I'll be ready in a sec. Got a little crazy in here." *Uh-oh. Busted. What are you going to do now? Don't forget your date with Ashwala. But what about Carly and Asia?! You have to get to your phone! Forget dinner!*

"Oh, right. Umm. I forgot to feed my cats. I have to go home."

"I'll come, and we can get dinner after." *Dude, get to your phone. Carly and Asia are probably DM'ing you right now! Drop Ashwala and grab your phone.*

"It's just I'm kind of in a hurry. I'm trying out this new food. Nellie's been throwing up."

"Oh no. Is she okay?

"Yeah. I just feed her little bits at a time." *PHONE, EDDIE! CARLY AND ASIA! SEX YOGA!*

"I can meet you when you're done?"

"It's ok, Ash. Gotta go. Text you tomorrow. BYE!"

I ran to my car and snatched my phone. Non-stop dings and pings. Hundreds of notifications. Likes, emojis, and DMs. Three hundred new followers in less than an hour. Tagged in FIVE different posts.

Stuck in a yoga high trance, I sat in my car and scrolled. I swiped up, down, left and right and counted my likes and new followers. *You flaked on Ashwala for this?! Go home, Eddie. You have to eat. Shower. You have two cats to feed. Stop staring at your phone! DM Carly! Find Asia on IG!*

I eventually found Asia and tapped on her profile. She had 782,000 followers and each photo, story, and selfie exuded the perfect combination of sexual and spiritual bliss. Waterfalls, sunsets, picturesque mountain and beach pics from around the world. All of them cropped and filtered with spiritual precision. Handstands on top of buildings, ski slopes, on top of cars, while racing down the freeway. She held Warrior One, Two, and Three wearing high-heel shoes and a bikini.

Model shots holding a new designer purse or wearing a chic pair of sunglasses. Candid side angle shots of her firm, rounded buttocks while she sipped an organic oat milk. Wheatgrass and juice selfies while taking a bubble bath. Seductive bedroom and pillow shots where she's lying on her bed and holding a Forward Fold. Pics where she's lying topless in the park with her dog, Yogini. Time-lapsed videos where she's moving through a yoga flow in a steam room. I tapped on the Follow icon and immediately felt a rush of sexual spirituality through my bones.

I tapped on Carly's page next and felt a powerful tingling and spiritual sensation emanate from my crotch. Carly's page was like a wild *Playboy* yoga magazine. Bathtub and shower yoga shots. Jungle shots. River and desert pics. Hundreds of booty and bikini pics and inspiring yoga thong shots. Waterfall thong shots. Celery juice thong shots. Egyptian pyramid thongs. Smoothie thongs. Coffee thongs and tea thongs. Puppy and cat thong shots. Eggs and thongs. Truffles and thongs. Pancakes and thongs. Salad and thongs. Cupcakes and thongs. Ice cream and thongs. She was a bona fide yoga supermodel with the hottest, most spiritual yoga page I had ever seen. It was a labyrinth concoction of yoga, *Playboy*, *Vogue*, and spirituality all tangled up into one IG yoga page. She had over a million followers...

1,162,000 followers, to be exact...

Her bio read...

"*Certified SSAFY Yoga Instructor. Always Spiritual and Always Sexy AF.*"

And right at the top of her IG page was the sweaty selfie Carly took with me after class. It had 65,000 likes, but the craziest part was when I eyeballed the pic, I had a six-pack. I don't know what filter she used. No idea how she created it, but I had a real-life six-pack. *Look at you! Your abs look super hot. You're going to be Insta-famous. You look so spiritual!* My body started to shake uncontrollably. The critical voices stormed back. *My half-naked body is on Carly's Instagram page! Don't you feel spiritual?! Your Instagram is going to explode. Let's say no one likes me?! She has to take it down! Are you nuts?! You will not tell her to take it down! That pic is staying! Eddie, stop looking at Instagram and go home and feed your cats! Text Ashwala. Meet her at the Almond Nut! NO! Take another selfie!*

I kept scrolling, spellbound by Carly's dazzling page. She had wavy blonde hair. Green eyes. A smile you could feel in your front pocket and smooth, angelic white skin. She was a virtuosic version of Yoga Wonder Woman, and her yoga superpower was Scorpion Pose. She held Scorpion on a yacht in Thailand. On top of a sea turtle in Hawai'i. At the airport. On top of a bus. On top of her car. Skyscrapers, hotel balconies, and bridges.

Carly always referred to her followers as "family" or "lovers" and made sure to respond to her followers' comments with a blue and purple heart emoji. 💙💜 She posted hundreds of black and white topless shots with the tiniest X's across her breasts. There was even a pic where she's upside down holding One-Handed Handstand. With her hair shielding her arm and hand, it looked like she was levitating in thin air.

I clicked on her IG stories next. There were hundreds of stories posted in the last twenty-four hours. Stories while getting a massage, eating chia seeds, or drinking chai tea. A story where she's sitting in an ice bath sucking on an ice cube. A green juice story, a facial story, beach stories, and an ice cream story. A comb-your-hair story, a put-on-organic-deodorant story, a shave-your-legs story, a manicure story, and a drinking-alkaline-water story where she's standing in her kitchen, in a bikini, drinking a bottle of water.

Eddie. Snap out of it! What about your cats?! Cats? Yes! Your cats! Nellie and Leo are starving! What about Carly and Asia? I want them to tag me again! GO HOME! Take a shower. Good idea! I can work on my shower selfies! NO SHOWER SELFIES!

Even at home, I couldn't resist the temptation and allure of Instagram. Pet my cat… INSTAGRAM! Make dinner… Check followers! Clip my nails… INSTAGRAM! Jump in the shower. Shower selfie! *Eddie! Listen to yourself. None of this is yoga! What happened to you? You had such a beautiful practice. Your breath has sounded amazing. Yuck, no one cares about the breath! You must speak to Vishypu. Go to your meditation den or meet Ashwala for a sound bath. SHOWER SELFIE!*

As I stepped out of the shower, I felt the return of the spiritual selfie sensations. I caught myself in the mirror and grabbed my phone. *Eddie, what are you doing? Who, me? Yes, you. Why did you grab your phone? My phone? What phone? The one in your hand! What are you doing? Oh, nothing. Are you taking an ab selfie? Me? No way. I'm just checking email. YOU'RE TAKING AN AB SELFIE! I'm just checking the yoga schedule… Wow, my abs look pretty good. I wish I had a selfie stick. I knew it! You're taking an ab selfie! OKAY, YES! I'M TAKING AN AB SELFIE!*

I tightened my abs and held my breath, praying for the tiniest glimpse of definition in my abdominals. *You're pathetic. Look at*

you. Taking an ab selfie. You disgust me! You have to dim the lights. Light some candles, dude! Six-packs always look better in the candle-light. I tucked in my belly. Nothing. No six-pack. *Damn it! Where did my six-pack go!? You never had one, loser. What filter did Carly use? I have all these new followers, and they think I have a six-pack.*

I tightened my belly and took a few more ab selfies. Snap-snap-snap. I opened Instagram and experimented with the different filters and effects. *Brightness, Eddie! Add some brightness! And some saturation! Try the Clarendon filter! No way, Lo-Fi! I think I see a two-pack. You did it! Yuck. Two-packs are for losers. A two-pack is better than nothing!* POST IT!

BZZZZZZZZZZZ.

My phone! It's Instagram! Open it!

It was a DM from Carly.

"Hey Eddie. Great work today! Our selfie just hit 90,000 likes. Super spiritual and sexy. Oh, and big news: I showed Sexy Swami Roge the selfie we took. He thought you were total SSAFY material and he would like to personally invite you to class tomorrow. We'll work on filters, selfies, and Handstand. Seventh Street and Wilshire. 9 AM. Come and don't bring a friend. Strictly invites only!!!"

Followed by a red sparkling heart emoji.

YES-YES-YES-YES! I'm going to SSAFY tomorrow! Sex Yoga! Their official guru invited me to class! Eddie, selfie! Post that two-pack!

I added a bit more brightness and hit POST. *Come on, baby! LIKE ME! LIKE ME!*

Thirty seconds passed. Zero likes. *Um, hello people? Just hold on, Eddie. They're coming. Promise. Why isn't anyone liking me!? Where are my likes!? No one likes a two-pack, you loser.*

A minute went by. Still nothing....

What the fuck, people? Like me! Your abs are gross, dude! HELLO? *Followers? Why aren't you liking me? What's wrong with my followers? It's not your followers. Two-packs suck. You picked the wrong filter! I'm going to delete it. Don't delete it! Just wait!*

BZZZ. My phone!

It's a like! Someone liked my abs! Come on, baby. More likes. More likes. Like me! Like my abs!

Like-Like-Like-Like-Like-Like-Like-Like-Like-Like...

My first ab selfie went on to receive over 750 likes, fifty-three heart emojis, and ninety-three comments. *Post another one! Would you* PLEASE *go to bed!* NO! *Post a story! An ab story! A shower selfie!* GO TO BED! It was close to two o'clock in the morning, and I couldn't stop. Scroll. Refresh. Like. Scroll. Refresh. Like. Follow. Scroll. Check DMs. Count followers. *Eddie, go to sleep! What is wrong with you? None of this is yoga. You need rest. You need to connect with your breath. Go to a meditation circle! Take a Savasana!* BREATHE!

POOF.

My phone battery died. NO! *What do I do? For the love of God, go to bed. Stop staring at your phone. I like you. We all like you. Your cats like you. I'm begging you. Just please go to sleep. Okay. Good night, Instagram. Good night followers. See you tomorrow, Carly and Asia!*

MY First DOWN DOG spank

I parked my Bird in front of the SSAFY studio. Two sexy yoginis, in high heels and matching G-string bikinis, stood like sentries by the door. They were busy tagging students, posting stories, and a Live Video Feed on Instagram. There were jumbo TV screens on the walls outside displaying the names of students scheduled for Carly's class, including a real-time follower count.

What the heck are you doing here?! They're not going to let you in. Turn around and go home. Go back to the Sanctuary! No way! Get your ass in there! You're on the guest list. Tell them the Swami invited you! Do you see how many followers these people have? There's no way I am getting into this class.

"Welcome to SSAFY! Are you ready to feel sexy and spiritual as fuck?"

"I'm here for Carly's class. I'm Eddie."

One of the yoginis looked at her iPad.

"Hmm, I don't see your name in the system. You're required to pre-book online. Carly's classes always sell out."

Eddie the loser can't get into class. Carly never told me to pre-book!

"Sorry, it's my first time here."

"It's okay. Do you have a six-pack?"

"A what?" *Ha, this loser? No way.*

"Your abs. Do you have a six-pack?"

"Um… no."

"It's required. Anyone who takes Carly's class must have a six-pack."

"I have a two-pack!"

"Eww. Gross. Sorry. That won't work. Carly has strict rules about her 9 AM on Saturdays. Everyone must have a six-pack. How about Instagram? Do you have 10,000 followers? What's your Insta?"

This is so pathetic. You're toast. Tell them you're friends with Carly!

"Well…uh… I actually have two accounts." *No, you don't, loser.*

"There's @eddiecohn. Don't look at that one. I barely use it, and I have @sexyeddieyoga." *Seriously? Do you hear how stupid you sound?*

"I don't see it here. Is it public? How many followers does it have?"

"I kinda lose track. Maybe 2,000? Could be three…"

"Yeah, I'm so sorry but to get into Carly's class, you need a six-pack and a minimum of 10,000 followers. Why don't you work on your abs and IG for a few weeks and come back when you're ready?"

Humiliated, I turned and walked away when one of the sexy yoginis grabbed my arm.

"Wait, did you say you're Eddie Cohn?"

"It's okay. I was just leaving…"

"Like THE Eddie Cohn on Carly's IG last night? That hot, sweaty selfie?!"

"Um, yeah…."

"I thought it was you! Wow. You looked so spiritual and hot. Even hotter in person. Roge put you on the list! Welcome to SSAFY! First time, right?"

"Yeah."

"YAY! First class selfie time!" The two yoginis leaned in, gave me a colossal squeeze, and snapped a "first class selfie" with me.

"K, we'll story this. This should totally help your Insta."

"Thanks!"

"Sorry for the confusion. We're not used to seeing people with less than 10,000 followers."

She means not used to seeing such a big loser!

"Go say hi to Asia at the front desk. She'll sign you in. Make sure you follow and tag SSAFY and all the students in class. Handles are on the screens. And don't worry, we'll hide your follower count. Oh, almost forgot. Do you prefer a pink Speedo or purple one?"

"A Speedo?"

"All new students get a free thong or Speedo. I'm thinking pink for sure."

I have to wear a Speedo?! DUH! You're going to look hot! You mean, pathetic! Stop torturing yourself. You don't belong in this place, Eddie! What would Ashwala and Vishypu say if they saw you in a Speedo?! Take the Speedo! Wear it! And stop being a wuss!

"I'll take the pink one."

"Excellent choice!"

Steam cascaded through the lobby as sexy yogis and yoginis prepared for class. Women in thongs and bikinis spraying oil all over their perfectly toned bodies. Dudes with six-pack abs doing chin-ups and push-ups, wearing nothing but little pink and purple Speedos. There was a tanning bed in one corner and a selfie photo booth in the other. A sun deck where students could lay out and a keg at the bar filled with organic kombucha for Keg Stands.

I peered over and saw Asia standing behind the counter. She wore the sexiest orange see-through tank top, a white bikini bottom, definitely no bra, and she was spraying massage oil on some of the guests.

"Asia!" Asia looked up. *Please remember me! Please-please-please!*

"Eddie! You made it!"

"Totally."

"Yay! FYI, I saw your follower count. It's pretty low so we asked Roge to put you on the list."

"Thanks, Asia. The girls up front told me you could hide my follower count?"

"Already done."

"Should I thank Roge for putting me on the list?"

"Not sure he'll make it to class, but you'll meet him soon. Promise!"

Tell her about your ab selfie!

"I took my first ab selfie last night."

"I saw! Already liked it. So spiritual."

"Sorry it was just a two-pack."

"That's okay. It was super sexy. What filter was that?"

"Clarendon and a little brightness."

"Nice."

"You think Carly can teach me how to get a six-pack?"

"Totally. She's such a pro. Picking the right filter is such an art when it comes to the six-pack. Come here and sign a few release forms. I'll walk you into the studio. I'm taking class, too. You have water, right? And a towel?"

"Yep."

"And your phone?"

"Of course."

"Great."

Asia walked me towards the studio when I noticed out of the corner of my eye, she kept looking at my saggy grey shorts. *UGH. Eddie. She hates them. Put the Speedos on, you loser. I don't wear Speedos! Those shorts are disgusting. So not sexy. I'm not wearing Speedos!*

"Eddie, where are the Speedos? They should have given you free ones. Please wear them."

"No, really, I'm ok. Maybe next class."

"If Roge sees you with those shorts on, he will go bananas."

"I really have to wear them?"

"Since Roge isn't here, I'll let it slide, but you'll have to next time. Roge is very strict on proper attire. We try to create as spiritual of an environment as possible inside the studio."

"Next time, promise."

"Try wearing them at home. You'll get used to them. AHH! I can't wait to practice with you!"

Asia opened the door, and a thick white cloud of steam gushed out of the room. It must have been at least 100 degrees inside the studio. *I'm going to die! How does anyone breathe in here?! There's no breathing at SSAFY! Then how the fuck does anyone do yoga in here? It's a sauna. I'm going to get heatstroke! Would you stop whining and get your ass in there!*

It was pitch black except for a few candles lined along the back wall of the room. I peeked around and saw the silhouette of two women kissing and giving each other a massage in the corner. A sexy yogini was taking yoga bicycle selfies, while another yogi was working on One-Handed Handstand in the middle of the room. Class hadn't even begun, and I was already sweating, feeling light-headed and, to my surprise, even a little aroused. *This place is weird, man. It's sweaty and gross. It's too* HOT. *It's like some weird sex yoga. Exactly! It's perfect.*

Asia looked at me, "You cool with the front row? Front row is best for selfies."

"Can they turn on the fan? It's hot in here, right?"

"DUH, it's supposed to be hot. When you have a room full of sexy yogis, it gets HOT."

"What's the temperature in here?"

"105 degrees… Don't worry. It'll get hotter… 115 is optimal for SSAFY."

115 degrees!? This is insane! Eddie, you can't do this. You can't do yoga in here. It's too dark. It's too hot! You're going to get a heart attack. Go to a sound bath. Eddie, shut the hell up! You are not leaving, and you're definitely not going back to your old loserville yoga studio. Look at this place! It feels like an orgy could start any second. Best yoga studio ever!

Asia and I put our mats down in the front row.

"There are selfie sticks and oil in the back."

"Where are the blocks?"

Asia laughed. "We banned blocks. Take your shirt off, get your selfie stick, do some yoga bicycles, and I'll be right back. Oh, and rub some of the SSAFY hot oil on your abs."

How am I going to do Triangle Pose without a block? Blocks are for losers! Stop asking so many stupid questions and do what Asia says!

I rubbed a drop of oil on my belly and biceps, and with a selfie stick in hand, walked back to my mat. I connected my phone, took my shirt off, and prepped with some yoga bicycles. Every few seconds, camera flashes went off. Like runway models at

Yoga Fashion Week, scantily clad sexy yogis and yoginis waltzed into class.

The anticipation grew as the packed room of yogis made their way to Selfie Sukhasana. An eighty-inch flat-screen TV displayed everyone's IG handle on the wall, ensuring students could tag their fellow sexy yogis.

A disco ball descended from the ceiling. Cardi B's "Bodak Yellow" exploded out of the speakers. Students stood, raised their selfie sticks in the air, and started dancing, twerking, and taking hot yoga dance selfies.

Asia returned to class cheering us on as the energy in the room escalated to a spiritual crescendo. As she walked, two yogis were rubbing oil all over her body while a cameraman chased beside her shooting video of her runway-type entrance.

Asia positioned herself next to me in Sukhasana. "Isn't this amazing? This room gets so spiritual when Carly teaches. Her 9 AM is by far the most spiritual class of the week."

"Incredible!"

"I hired a photographer for class. I need some new pics for social. I'll tell him to take some shots of you!"

The mirrors were already covered with steam. Sweat was flying and dripping everywhere. Dancing, more screams, and selfies as more yogis and yoginis twerked and rubbed oil on their bodies. My eyes burned as sweat seeped into my eyes. I started to feel even more light-headed. *I can't breathe! I can't do this. I'm going to pass out. It's too hot! Eddie! Drink some damn water and stop whining. It's too hot in here! I need air!*

"Asia, can I step outside? Just for a second?" *What the fuck did I just tell you?! You are not leaving!*

"Class is about to start."

"I'm so hot."

"Of course you are. That's why we invited you."

"No really, it's so hot in here."

"You'll get used to it. It's normal to feel like this in your first class."

"I feel kind of dizzy."

"Trust me."

Asia grabbed her water bottle and poured ice-cold water over my body. She pulled an ice cube out and rubbed it on my back and chest. She leaned in and whispered, "You're going to do great. Let's get a quick selfie in. We gotta get your numbers up."

"Thank you, Asia."

"Next time, you BETTER wear a Speedo, or Roge will kill both of us."

No one was taking Child's Pose or Savasana. No wimpy yoga stretches, no blocks or bolsters. No sounds of "Om." Not a single "Namaste" or "Shanti." Not even a breath. Just selfies, dancing, texting, DMs, and Handstands. As the lights went out, steam blew down from the overhead vents. Britney Spears' "I'm A Slave 4 You" pumped through the speaker system. Red and blue laser lights shimmered off the mirrored walls, and when the door opened, the whole class rose to their feet, grabbed their phones, and screamed at the top of their lungs, "CARLY-CARLY-CARLY!"

Asia yelled out, "DON'T FORGET TO TAG EVERYONE, SEXY YOGIS! HANDLES ARE ON THE SCREEN!"

It was a rock concert atmosphere. Screaming, flashing lights, yogis jumping up and down, cell phones in the air. As the music grew even louder, the room felt like it was about to explode. When I looked up, Carly was standing in the doorway wearing sunglasses, a leather collar around her neck, ten-inch black heels, leather yoga pants, and a black leather tank top. She held a whip/yoga strap in one hand and a selfie stick in the other. She was part Margot Robbie, part Bella Hadid, part Aphrodite and the tiniest bit of a yoga teacher. She signed a few autographs, whipped a few students with her strap, and took selfies as she slowly made her way to the front of class. Carly stepped up onto an elevated stage, put her headset on, and prepared to guide us on our hour-long journey of sexual spirituality.

"Good morning sexy yogis!"

More cheers and screams.

"You all look so sexy and spiritual today! Love the energy. Place your hands on your body and give yourselves a massage. Feel the sexual spirituality in the room. Now open up Instagram and look at how many followers you have. Ask yourself, what can you do today so when you walk out of here, you'll feel more sexually spiritual and have more followers? The TV screens have everyone's handles. Lots of stories and selfies, yogis. I want to be tagged in at least 100 stories today!"

The music grew even louder. More camera flashes and loud screams.

"ARE YOU READY TO FEEL SEXY AND SPIRITUAL AS FUCK?!"

"YEAH!!!!!!!"

"I CAN'T HEAR YOU! ARE YOU READY TO FEEL SEXY AND SPIRITUAL AS FUCK?!"

"YEAH!!"

"Selfie Sukhasana giveaway time! Grab your selfie stick and start taking those Sukhasana Selfies. We'll start to move more explosively but for now, hold your phone, feel the energy from your phone and explore your sexy selfies. Maybe rub some of the SSAFY oil on your abs or lean over towards your neighbor's mat and take a selfie together. When you're done with your Sukhasana selfies, pick the one that makes you feel the most sexually spiritual. Add a little filter, tag SSAFY, and post it. Filter of the day is Lo-Fi, lovers. Whoever's selfie gets the most likes will get a free SSAFY açaí bowl. We'll count the likes after class!"

Over the next sixty minutes, we were her yoga slaves as Carly guided us through a yoga class filled with an obscene amount of sexual spirituality. There was grunting, groaning, and sweat splashing across the mirrors. Screams and twerks, booty shakes, and Handstands. A few students poured candle wax on each other while a few yogis did nothing but yoga bicycles. Students held Forearm Plank and took Plank selfies while others took selfies and made out in Crescent Pose. Through it all, Carly walked around the room, assisting us on our own unique sexual yoga journey. No cues or comments about alignment. Nothing about feet positioning, lifting the chest, or about the breath.

"Okay, sexy yogis, let's open it up to Selfie Warrior Two. If you have two phones, now is your time to work on those Double Warrior Two selfies! Everyone looks super spiritual."

The roomful of yogis reached their arms wide and made their way to Selfie Warrior Two. Within seconds, my biceps and traps started to feel the burn, and my legs shook uncontrollably as sweat gushed into my eyes. My heart beat faster, and I started to get lightheaded. My body was beginning to feel dehydrated as the voices returned. *It's too hot! I can't take it. I need to get out of here! When can I take Child's Pose? I need a Child's Pose! NO! You don't take Child's Pose, you wimp! I need my breath back. You don't breathe either! Why isn't Carly talking about the breath? The breath doesn't matter. No one in here is taking Child's Pose! I can't breathe! Who cares! I need water! Damn it, Eddie! Stop crying and hold Selfie Warrior Two! I want my old yoga practice back. Grow some balls and stay in Warrior Two!*

As the voices spun out of control, I put my phone down and tried to refocus my awareness on my breath. I didn't care what Asia or Carly said, I needed my old yoga practice back. *Just breathe, Eddie. You're okay. You're doing great. Remember what Vishypu says. Breathe. Focus on your.... Eddie, what the hell are you doing!? Grab your phone, NOW! Are you breathing? Yes, I am breathing. I'm about to pass out. I need to breathe. It's too hot in here. No one in here is breathing! I don't care! Carly never told you to breathe. And where is your phone? Carly never told you to put your phone down. Open your eyes! She's coming! Who? CARLY! I have to breathe. YOU AREN'T SUPPOSED TO BE THINKING OF YOUR BREATH, YOU IDIOT! Open your eyes! Carly is right in front of you! No, she isn't. YES, SHE IS! She's going to kill you! Open your eyes!*

"Hi, Eddie."

You're in so much trouble.

"Where's your phone?"

"Uh…"

"Are you breathing?"

"Who me? No way."

"It looks like you were breathing."

"Nah. Breathing is for sissies."

"I am pretty sure I saw you take a conscious breath."

"Okay, yes! I took a breath."

"There is no conscious breathing at SSAFY!"

"I'm really sorry, Carly."

Carly reached down, grabbed my phone, and handed it back to me. She opened my water bottle, pulled out an ice cube, and gently skimmed the ice cube across my chest.

"How does that feel?"

"So much better."

"Does that feel spiritual?"

"So spiritual."

"Are you breathing?"

"I hate the breath."

"Eddie, I'll let it slide this time, but you never ever put your phone down, and next time I see you in here, you better be wearing a Speedo. If Roge saw you in here without a Speedo, he'd pull you out of class."

"I'll never put my phone down or breathe again, and I'll always wear a Speedo."

"Promise?" She glided the ice cube down my belly and then placed it on my lips. Carly lifted her phone, leaned in, took a selfie as she used her tongue to put the ice cube in her mouth.

"I swear!"

"You want me to post this?"

"Please post it. Please."

"You promise to wear a Speedo to class?"

"Yes, I promise. I'll wear a Speedo."

Carly went back on the mic and yelled out to class, "Hop, jump, or fly and let's meet in Selfie Downward Facing Dog. Amazing work, sexy yogis. I just checked Instagram and our SSAFY account already has 500 new followers! Take a sip or a selfie. Follower counts are looking good, lovers!"

As I held Dog, my mind wandered toward some of the deeper, more spiritual questions of my yoga practice. Why hadn't Vishypu or Ashwala ever poured water on my body or rubbed ice cubes on my chest? Why hadn't Vishypu ever suggested I should wear tight-fitting Speedos? Why had I been focusing so much attention on the breath? Was Child's Pose actually an enormous waste of time? Why had I never learned how to take selfies in a yoga class, and why was I just learning about the value of Instagram?

Carly pranced her way back towards the stage. "Okay, sexy yogis. Sexy inversion time. We're going to work on One-Handed Selfie Handstand. This posture is super hot on Insta right now, averaging more likes than any other yoga posture. Grab your phones and gather around."

Asia took my hand. "We need to get up close!" Everyone hustled towards the stage and huddled in as Carly effortlessly lifted herself up into Handstand. "Okay, yogis. Take out your phones. Tag and story me. Whoever's story gets the most views will receive a one-hour free tanning session at Sexy Yogi Tan!" Students whipped out their phones and started taking stories and selfies.

"Belly in, abs tight. Once you have your core engaged and you feel stable, gently lift one hand off the ground and grab your phone and selfie stick." Like a trapeze artist and with barely any effort, Carly raised one hand off the mat, grabbed her selfie stick, and began to take selfies. IN ONE-HANDED HANDSTAND!

"STORY ME, YOGIS!" Carly screamed into her headset. "Notice how my face is in ideal selfie position and how my eyes are looking directly at my phone. My legs and core are on fire!"

A student yelled out, "I just storied you! I have 300 views!"

Another student screamed, "I have 600 views! I get the free tan! I win!"

Someone else hollered, "No way, I do! I'm up to 800 views!"

Carly came down from her Selfie Handstand. "We'll tabulate the views after class. Winner gets an email tonight. It's your turn, lovers. You can work on Handstand without the selfie. If you have to use the wall for support, that's okay. If you need my help, wave me over. You can always hang out in Selfie Plank, do yoga bicycles, or maybe post on TikTok. Whatever your body needs."

Everyone dispersed back to their mats and worked on Handstand, ab selfies, or scrolled through Instagram. As I worked on Selfie Forearm Plank, one of Carly's sexy yoga assistants walked in, holding a large bucket of towels.

Carly got back on the mic, "After your final Handstand, everyone meet me in Down Dog. Monica is walking around the room with ice-cold organic PABA-free lavender-infused towels. You'll find one at the corner of your mat. Place it on your forehead for a refreshing cool-down selfie. Maybe around your neck or your pubic bone to help your body cool off. Then one final Dog, yogis!"

Asia snagged me by the arm. "Eddie, this is the best part of class. Carly walks around and spanks and whips everyone with her strap! In Down Dog!"

"She's going to do what!?"

"It's so hot. Our Instagram is going to go crazy!"

George Michael's "I Want Your Sex" blasted through the speakers as I held one last Dog. Everybody pressed their buttocks high in the air, prepping for the sexual spiritual torture Carly was about to inflict on us. Wearing a black eye mask and long leather gloves, Carly walked around the room like a panther stalking its prey. I could hear the sound of a whip smack the floor and her hand spanking one sexy yogi after another followed by loud screams, groans, and grunts. *What the hell am I doing in here?! It's like some sick yoga sex camp! It's yoga heaven!* S&M *Yoga, baby! Your Gaba is going to freaking explode! Get ready! This can't be yoga. Tell me this isn't yoga! Hell yeah this is yoga! I don't think I can do this. Yes, you can! I just want to breathe and lie in Savasana.* ARE YOU A FUCKING IDIOT? *This is the best yoga day ever, and you're acting like a sissy.*

I closed my eyes and anxiously waited for the spiritual ecstasy of my first Down Dog Spanking. I pressed my hips high in the air. I waited and waited... Finally....

WHACK!

Holding a whip and drenched in sweat, Carly stood directly behind me with a devilish grin on her face. She leaned in close right behind my ear and whispered, "You want me to do that again, Eddie?" *Yes! Harder! Harder! Spank me!* STOP IT! *What is wrong with you? Oh, shut up, loser Eddie! Carly, yes, spank me! Spank me hard!*

In a soft whisper, she asked me again. "One more time?"

I nodded my head up and down, closed my eyes, and held my nasty Down Dog a little longer. I pressed my thigh bones back and anxiously waited for the spiritual punishment of another Down Dog Spanking.

SMACK!

She used her whip this time. I looked over towards Asia who was pointing her phone directly at me. She captured the yoga whipping LIVE for IG. *Eddie! You're going to be famous! You just got whipped Live on Instagram! My mother is going to kill me.*

Carly leaned in and put her lips right behind my ear, "You're a dirty little yogi."

Asia grabbed my hand, "You looked scorching hot. Didn't it feel amazing?"

My body was still shaking. I could barely open my mouth and gasped, "I feel so spiritual."

"I storied everything! You just passed 5,000 followers!"

Carly walked towards the front of class, raised her arms up high, and prepared the room for one final group selfie before she let us go.

"Get in close everyone! One spiritual group selfie for Instagram! Give your fellow sexy yogi a tag and a sweaty hug."

Asia grabbed my hand and led me to the center of the room.

"Don't forget your phone and selfie stick! Group selfie time!"

We huddled in close and held our selfie sticks high. I was engulfed by ninety half-naked sweaty bodies, and as I glanced around the room, not only did I feel sexually spiritual, I was convinced I would never take a yoga class at The Yoga Sanctuary again. No more Vishypu or sound baths. No more meditation circles or silly full moon events. I was reinvigorated by the sweat, thongs, and Speedos. I connected with Carly's no-holds-barred approach to teaching. The way she moved her body and how sexy and spiritual she looked teaching in all leather. The way her hands felt on my body when she spanked me. How she encouraged me to hold my phone and think about Instagram in each posture.

There were cheers, screams, hugs, and tags. As Carly raised her phone high and captured one final group selfie, the critical voices returned. *What about Savasana!? What about the last cleansing breath? Why isn't anyone lying still? You need the Sanctuary! This isn't yoga!*

Carly clapped her hands. "Great work today, sexy yogis! Don't forget to keep on tagging. Remember lovelies, we have a workshop next week on belfies and next week is Skone's one-week immersive on how to hold Handstand on top of buildings and moving objects. There's the workshop on Down Dog selfies. Misty's Bathtub Yoga intensive has just a few spots left. Lots of exciting stuff happening at the studio. If you're interested in the twenty-hour TT, talk to me or Asia. Whether you want to be a teacher, an influencer, or you're just looking to expand your Instagram presence, it's a great way to feel more spiritual! Put your selfie sticks away. Love you, yogis! See you on Instagram!"

The room smelled of sex. Sweat and bodily fluid covered the floor. A sexy yogi assistant was busy wiping down the mirrors while a sexy yogini rolled out a keg for Kombucha keg stands. As I walked out of the studio, Asia ran after me and gave me a post-yoga class hug.

"SOOOOOOOO, do you feel amazing?"

"Wow, that was some yoga class."

"You look super-spiritual. How is your yoga high!?"

"I feel so high." *You mean aroused, you perv.*

"SSAFY has the best yoga highs!"

"My Gaba levels feel awesome."

Asia looked at me, confused. "Your what?"

"My Gaba." *Eddie, would you shut up about stupid Gaba! Asia could care less about Gaba.*

"Hmm, not sure what that is but did you see?! Carly posted it! It already has 50,000 likes!"

"What has 50,000 likes?"

"Your ass, Eddie! The Down Dog Spank!"

"WHAT?!"

"Carly tagged your ass! The SSAFY community loves your ass. Look!"

Asia opened Carly's profile. Right at the top was a photo of me bent over in Dog with Carly's hand swatting my keister. The lighting. The filters. The continuous looping effect; all shot with spiritual perfection. It was technically called a "boomerang," but in just a few minutes, the spank had amassed over 80,000 views, 53,000 likes, and I was over 7,000 followers! *I have to take that down! Are you insane?! Your ass is trending! What the heck is the matter with you?! I have to untag my ass! She has to take that down! You will not take that down!*

"So proud of you."

"Thanks, Asia."

"Have you met Skone? You two have to meet." Asia looked outside to the sun deck.

"Skone, get over here! I want you to meet someone."

Wearing nothing but a purple thong with the letters SSAFY stitched on the backside, Skone spun down from Handstand and strolled inside. He had spiked blond hair, nipple rings, and tattoos that covered his arms and chest.

Skone leaned in and gave Asia a hug. "Yo, Asia. Such a great class. Carly nailed it today. I just hit 600 K on IG. Where is she? I wanna get a story with her."

"Wait, I want you to meet Eddie. He just took class."

"Dude, I saw that Down Dog Spank. You killed it today. That boom with you and Carly is sick!"

Asia chimed in. "Skone, it's his first class!"

"No way."

"He's never been to SSAFY before!"

Skone gave me a high-five, "You're a fucking natural, bro."

"You have to take Skone's workshop this weekend. He is the Spiderman of SSAFY. Skone, maybe you can give Eddie some tips on Handstand. We're really trying to get his spirituality levels higher."

"Totally. Come take my workshop. Maybe this week we can try out Balcony Handstand. I'll spot you. You'll be holding Handstand in no time."

Skone gave Asia another hug and raised his hand towards me for a high-five. "Gotta blow, guys. Asia, have you seen Roge or Gordo? We were going to shoot some ab videos for YouTube."

"Gordo has a Plank workshop going on in studio B. Not sure about Roge. I'm sure he's floating around somewhere."

Skone strutted back outside and leaped into another Handstand. Asia looked at me and said, "K, I gotta get in a few shower selfies before I teach the next class. Have you taken a shower selfie before?"

"Don't think so."

"Gosh, I wish Roge was around. He could show you."

"How 'bout Skone?"

"He's not certified in Shower Yoga. Misty isn't here, either. It's okay. Just take a few ab selfies and come see me after. I want to tell you about our promotions. We have a discount for new students with over 7,000 followers. You'll receive $50 off the first two months, two free Speedos, a wheatgrass shot, and a premium selfie stick, plus all workshops are thirty percent off during the first year of your membership. Go shower. See you after."

Candles shimmered throughout the locker room as low-thumping electro dance music pumped out of the 50-inch JBL speakers. Mirrors covered the walls and ceiling. *Dude. Get your phone out! Post-class selfie time. More selfies? Duh! YES! Take the selfie! This place is weird. Everyone's topless. There are mirrors on the ceilings! No one talks about the breath! Would you stop about the breath! SSAFY doesn't care about breathing! This can't be yoga! This is yoga! Asia didn't know what Gaba is. Who the fuck cares about Gaba!*

The negative voices crept back, but I knew I couldn't let Asia down. When I caught a glimpse of my abdominals in the mirrors, I turned my body, dropped my gaze, and flexed my abs. I whipped my phone out and immersed myself in a post-yoga class selfie frenzy. Snap-snap-snap.

A sexy yogi wearing just a towel around his waist whirled in from behind me and photobombed my selfie. I turned around, and just when I was about to tell him off, I realized I'd seen that face before. The long hair. The cleanly shaven chest. The sculpted cheeks, the white teeth, and perfect smile. The fake tan. It was

Roge! Roge looked over and saw my phone face down by my side. *It's* ROGE! *Get your phone! Take a selfie! Tag him! Quick! Put on the Speedo! AHHH!! Roge is going to kick your Speedo-less ass.*

"Dude. Rule 1 at SSAFY. Phone is never down. And bro, where are the Speeds? No one is allowed inside the studio without a thong or Speedo. No exceptions."

"Really sorry. It's my first time here."

"You always carry two Speeds. One for class and a clean one for the post-class thong selfies."

"It won't happen again."

Roge looked annoyed and then took a longer look at my face. "Lift your shirt. I wanna see those abs."

"Wait, you what?"

'The abs. I want to see your abs." *Is he serious? Yes, lift your damn shirt! Listen to Roge!*

"You want to see my abs?"

Roge was losing his patience. "Yes, yes. Come on. Let's go. I wanna see those abs. Did they check your abs at the door?" *You're busted. He's going to see your flabby pathetic stomach and kick you out of here.*

Roge didn't move. He just stood there staring, waiting. I slowly lifted my shirt over my head. As Roge took a quick peek at my abs, his face transformed from a piercing scowl to a celebratory smile.

"You're the dude Carly took that sick selfie with at Sanctuary. I thought it was you! I love it when they crash that place!"

"You saw that?"

"That was super spiritual as fuck."

"Thanks! It was my first selfie."

Roge looked at me, shocked, and said, "Your first selfie?! No way."

"Yep."

"Dude, you're killing it. That was total pro."

"You're Roge, right?"

"Sexy Swami, Roge. One and only. Welcome to my house. Home of Shower Yoga, the Yoga Strip Show, Skyscraper Handstand Workshops, the most spiritual abs and influencers in the world, and pretty soon, SSAFY Austin."

"Namaste, Roge. I'm Eddie."

"Nama what?! No-no-no! We don't ever say Namaste at SSAFY."

I brought my hands together at my heart and bowed my head. Roge smacked me across the top of the head.

"What the hell are you doing? You don't bow the head. Dude, get your face back to selfie position. It's selfie time. Come on."

Roge untied the towel around his waist to reveal a leopard patterned thong. Roge gave me a bear hug squeeze and hoisted his phone in the air. His hips pressed up against my thigh as we prepared for our first selfie together. *Yes! Yes! Selfie with Roge! I'm about to take a selfie with THE SEXY SWAMI!*

As we prepped for our selfie, Roge paused and took a long look at my face. "You're Ashwala's friend!"

Roge remembered me!

"Dude, I've been trying to get Ash over here and out of that dumb Sanctuary. You two are total SSAF material."

"Yeah, I'm not sure she'd be into this kind of yoga."

"Bro, we're way more yoga than boring Sanctuary. The analytics on IG prove the yoga highs and follower counts at SSAFY exceed any other studio. Carly. Skone. Asia. That's as spiritual as you get."

"Ashwala probably connects with Vishypu's teaching style."

"Come on! He has no followers. Freaking Vishy doesn't even know how to take an ab selfie. I'm way more spiritual than Vishypu. Let's take a selfie and send it to Ash!" *If you take this selfie, Ashwala will kill you. Would you get out of here! Do not take the selfie!*

"You know, I think I got in enough selfies for today."

Roge looked at me with disgust and said, "Excuse me!?"

"I've taken like fifty selfies."

"Bro. No offense, but you really gotta up the selfie game. Your numbers are still way too low for SSAFY. If other students knew you were in here, they would freak out. We need to get you over that 50 K threshold pronto. Put on the Speeds, and let's send a selfie to your girl, Ashwala."

"How 'bout I take a shower and…"

Roge jumped with enthusiasm and interrupted me. "Great idea! We'll take a shower selfie and send it to her! Oh man, you're going to love the SSAF showers. Have you taken a shower selfie? Water trickling down your body. Steam everywhere. So spiritual."

"I don't know, Roge."

"We'll take one together." *Is he serious?! He wants to take a shower with me?! YES! Take a shower! Take off your stupid shorts and jump in the shower!*

Roge turned the water on and continued with his shower selfie pitch. "Ed-D! We got 4K cameras installed, 360-degree panoramic selfies, waterproof phones inside, superzooms. You can go Live from the shower. Boomerangs while you shampoo your hair. The best shower gel for those sudsy shower selfies."

"Roge, really, I don't know. A selfie together… in the shower?"

"YES!"

"With no clothes on?"

"No! Bro. Keep the Speeds on. They're our biggest sponsor. They pay me big bucks when I tag them in the shower. Let's do this!"

Roge could sense my apprehension.

"Ed-D! Ashwala is going to love it." *Ashwala will kill you!*

"I really think I know how to shower."

"Bro, it's not just a shower." Roge wouldn't let up. "There's a real art form to the shower selfie. Using the proper filter, the perfect lighting with all the steam."

"It's just Asia is waiting for me."

"You can't flake out on the shower selfie. It's a vital part of the practice."

"How about next time?"

"Promise?"

"I swear."

"K. I'll sign you up for Misty's Shower and Bathtub Yoga workshop. I don't want you falling behind. She's the only instructor at SSAFY certified in shower selfies. She's the bomb. Anything you need to help you feel more spiritual, SSAFY has you covered."

"Thanks, Roge."

"Stoked you're here, Ed-D! Your spirituality is going to freaking explode! Welcome to the SSAFY family." Roge put his hands on my shoulders, snapped a quick selfie, gave me a gentle spank on the ass, and walked towards the door. "Say hi to Ash for me! We gotta get you two in here for my next selfie workshop!"

"For sure, Roge."

"And tell Asia I'm comping your workshops this first month. All on me, buddy! I see serious spiritual potential in you! We're gonna make you feel spiritual AS FUCK! SSAF baby! Remember to post some selfies and tag SSAFY!"

Like a sexy yogi Speedy Gonzalez, Roge and his leopard patterned thong zipped out of the locker room. I didn't know what to do next. Check Instagram? Post an ab selfie? Work on shower selfies or run out of there as fast as I could. *Take the damn shower selfie! Roge was about to take a shower selfie with you, and you ruined it! Would you put the damn Speedos on?! Eddie! RUN! GO! Get out of this psycho yoga studio! Call Ashwala and go to a sound bath! This isn't yoga! Go back to the Sanctuary! Get out of here! No way! Time to join SSAFY!*

As my head spun from indecision, I wondered, who was this man who was turning the yoga world upside down? Was it possible that Instagram and a skimpy bathing suit were all you need to feel spiritual? Where did SSAFY, Roge, Carly, and Asia come from? How did Roge turn a quaint little yoga studio into a spiritually charged yoga sex den? I had to know.

CHAPTER 6
SSAFY AND THE BIRTH OF THE SPIRITUAL EIGHT

It was 2015. Netflix, Snapchat, Amazon Prime, FB, IG, filters, and emojis were all the rave. Millions of people walking in the middle of city streets and texting at the same time, working out while taking selfies, posting a filtered #nofilter pic while driving. And in the midst of the tech craze was Roge, a retired adult film actor turned yogi.

Like most adult film stars approaching forty, Roge had lost his on-screen flair and mojo. On the last day of his final shoot, the cast and crew threw a celebratory bon-voyage party for Roge, one of the leaders in the porn industry. When fans and fellow actors asked him what he had planned for retirement, to everyone's surprise, Roge told the crowd he signed up for a twenty-hour yoga teacher training program on YouTube. Roge was tired of the grueling schedule, the late nights, and the strain on his impeccable body. He was ready to slow down and thought what better way than to become a certified yoga teacher.

After completing his TT on YouTube with Johanna, a local fashion model turned yogi, Roge got a gig teaching three times a week at Earthtown Yoga. Within two short months, Roge was already garnering a small following of students, mostly women and gay men, who responded to his baritone voice, his perfect hair, and laidback teaching style. Yet despite the slow growth in popularity, Roge was still feeling unsatisfied. Compared to the grunts, the groans, and body-to-body contact in adult film, teaching yoga lacked a certain pizzazz and wow factor he craved. Being zen and chill may have been a good concept, but deep down, Roge knew that yoga lacked something. Momentum. Bravado. Cameras. Pelvic Thrusts. Moans. Less Clothing. Sex!

One evening while whitening his teeth and watching old porn videos from his massive collection, Roge had an idea. What if he added a little sex to yoga and taught class wearing a thong? What if he rubbed massage oil on students? What if he played hip-hop or dance music and took selfies in class? Would the yoga community be open to such radical ideas?

The next evening while sipping on a mint cacao chip smoothie at Cafe Thankful, Roge overheard a group of fellow yoga teachers complaining about their students and dwindling class sizes. Despite the new tech developments happening, yoga studios still clung to a no cell phone and selfie policy, and with that... attendance rates took a dramatic hit. Students preferred phones, selfies, and Netflix over slowing down and focusing on the breath. While a few desperate teachers tried to incorporate social media by posting Sukhasana and Hands-At-The-Heart pics, nothing could escape the harsh truth that yoga was too dull to compete with the new fast-paced culture. Nibbling on a cacao seed, Roge wondered if now more than ever, yoga could use a little tap-tap on the ass. A little spice and sizzle. A "rebranding" of sorts, embracing sex and social media to help revitalize the ancient practice and draw students back to their mat.

Throughout the week, Roge tried out some of his cutting-edge ideas. He brought in a smoke machine and took smoke screen selfies with students as they arrived at the studio. Roge hooked up two 100 watt K2 speakers and a subwoofer and hired a local DJ to play some of the hottest dance tracks in class. He added balloons, a disco ball, and strobe lights, creating a nightclub atmosphere. Once class began, he took non-stop selfies with students and shared the A and B Flow series Live on Facebook. Roge even gave students body-to-body adjustments in the Standing Postures. However, the most dramatic shift had to have been the dress code. Roge ditched the sweat pants and t-shirt and wore nothing but a low-cut thong and promised students an oil massage or extra long "adjustment" in Savasana for anyone who wore a bikini or Speedo.

Over the next month, Roge's popularity grew as he implemented even more ideas: tighter-fitting thongs and an elevated stage at the front of class. Keg stands, stripper poles, body shots in Savasana, hip-hop on Fridays, and a fan favorite; the Whip Cream and Feather Flow. Pretty soon, his 6 AM classes were selling out with students eager to feel the spiritual essence of Roge's new style of yoga. The studio owner asked Roge if he'd be willing to take on a few more classes at night, but Roge had loftier goals. Roge majored in marketing before dropping out of college and had a sense his ideas were too grandiose for one small studio in Santa Monica. Deep down, Roge knew he was scratching the surface on an idea that, if in the right hands, could reshape the yoga community and make him a star.

Roge was still a newcomer in the yoga community, so he reached out to his YouTube teacher and shared some of his intentions. Johanna immediately resonated with this new approach and started teaching all of her YouTube classes in a thong bikini. Pretty soon, her YouTube channel morphed from 800 to over 200,000 subscribers, proving Roge's suggestions were revolutionary. Johanna invited Roge to join her at an upcoming yoga conference which she believed would be the perfect backdrop for Roge to present this spiritual new incarnation of yoga.

Each year, the yoga community held its American Spirituality Yoga Conference, where attendees talked about the latest trends in yoga. Studio owners, yoga apparel companies, creators of yoga accessories, gurus, and some of the most popular yoga teachers came together to discuss all things yoga. The conference was typically an empowering event held each year in Tulum, Mexico, but with class attendance dragging and studio owners losing money, many attendees couldn't afford the trip to Mexico. In 2016, the conference was moved to a Holiday Inn in Las Vegas, a couple of miles off the strip.

Johanna could sense the energy at this year's conference was more tumultuous than in previous years. Despite the early morning flow and meditation circle, teachers were discouraged by the changes happening in the yoga community. Students would leave class early and skip Savasana to get back to their phones.

Students begged to take selfies in Happy Baby or cried when the teacher demanded everyone put their phones away. Stories of students having panic attacks when teachers suggested a digital detox, and the more teachers and studio owners said "no" to tech, class sizes continued to drop.

While a few teachers held out hope that more traditional ideas could bring a newfound interest back to the beloved practice, most attendees believed nothing could be done to compete with the addictive allure of tech.

Halo, a herbal tea mixologist from Rhode Island, refused to believe changes were necessary. "It's not the yoga that needs to evolve, yogis. It's the students. They must learn to turn off their phones. To tap into the breath and ignore the toxic stimulants of tech."

Johanna and Roge sat in the corner, listening to the ongoing back and forth. Jo leaned over and whispered to Roge, "Are you going to tell them or what?"

Looking a bit unsure, Roge said, "Maybe this isn't such a good idea."

Ignoring Roge, Johanna stood up and threw out one of his ideas. "How about TV screens on the walls? We keep track of student's Instagram following in class."

"NOOOOO!"

"DJs in class!"

"NEVER!"

Jo shrugged and quickly sat back down. Roge looked at Jo and whispered, "I told you."

Cupid, an ex-GQ model turned yogi, had a suggestion. "I'm friends with one of the Kardashians. Maybe I can get them to do weekly yoga Live on IG?"

"The Kardashians are not true yoginis!"

"Why don't we just allow texting in class?" Cherish, a senior teacher from New York suggested.

Shalamay, an elixir store owner from Santa Monica, jumped up from her chair.

"Cherish! How can you say that? The yoga room is a sacred space. There's no technology in the yoga room!"

Misty, an ex-swimsuit model, replied, "Let's just drop Savasana."

"You don't just drop Savasana."

"Okay. Then we make classes shorter. Thirty minutes. One minute of Savasana."

"You need at least an hour to experience the healing effects of a yoga class."

Misty offered another idea. "Netflix in class?"

The entire room screamed, "NO!"

Roge leaned over to Johanna. "Misty has some good ideas. I like her."

Skyler, a studio owner from Portland, had experienced a fifty percent drop-off in class size from the previous year. She was on the verge of closing her studio until she started to wear black leather yoga pants and high heel shoes when she teaches class. She stood up and tried to offer some perspective.

"I think it's time to consider making some adjustments to the practice. It'll still be yoga. I wear leather pants when I teach. Now my students tell me they feel a deeper connection to their yoga. And who cares if students want to take a selfie in Chair Pose."

Johanna chimed in. "Maybe we offer selfie workshops? And if we allow Instagram, then students won't skip Savasana."

Skyler agreed. "Yeah, I mean, is Savasana really that necessary?"

With disgust, Shalamay yelled out, "People! No leather and no Instagram! And as a reminder, Savasana is the primary reason why we practice yoga."

Roge looked at Jo, took a deep breath, and then stood up. "Yogi bros. Ladies. Look, technology isn't going away. We need to embrace our devices and bring a little sizzle to yoga. Make it more fun and exciting. A selfie during class could be just what students need. I've been taking selfies with students instead of Savasana, and everyone seems to dig it."

Shantise, a wheatgrass distributor from South Carolina, looked at Roge with confusion. "So no Savasana in your class?"

Roge stood there with a proud smile and said, "Nope. Got rid of it."

"You take selfies instead?"

"Smoke machine selfies to be exact."

Ashwala, couldn't believe what she was hearing and spoke up.

"Roge, I've been hearing some rumblings about your new class style at Earthtown."

"You should come take my class. You'd love the Feather Flow."

Shantise look intrigued. "Feather flow?"

With a proud grin, Roge tried to explain, "It's totally spiritual. I have everyone in Dog and then I…"

Ashwala quickly interrupted, "Roge. You're a new attendee."

"Yep, first time."

"And how long have you been teaching?"

"Almost two months."

"The yoga room isn't a breeding ground for sex and selfies, Roge. Texting inside the yoga room and this Feather Flow are a terrible idea. And I think I read somewhere that you're a porn star. You're definitely not a true yogi."

Roge glared at Ashwala. "EX-porn star."

More yogis piped in. "Roge, you're gross."

"How did a porn star get into teaching yoga?!"

Roge was losing his patience. "EX-PORN STAR!"

"Did you even take a 200-hour training?"

"I did a twenty-hour on YouTube with Johanna, right here."

"That's pathetic."

Johanna leaped from her chair, "You're pathetic!"

"You and Roge both are!"

Johanna wouldn't let up. "Roge is way more spiritual than any of you. His classes are blowing up right now! He has whip cream, bubble baths, DJs, a selfie booth!"

"SELFIE BOOTHS ARE NOT YOGA!!!"

Vishypu, a yearly participant at the conference, had been standing quietly in the back of the room listening and observing.

"Roge. All of you. The yoga community needs yogis like us now more than ever. We can't succumb to the technological tendencies of our society. Yoga is first and foremost about the breath. It's about community and being more mindful."

Roge disagreed. "Oh please, Vishypu. No one cares about the breath."

The bickering continued for hours with no solution in sight. Everyone dispersed and went to an evening meditation or the monthly sound bath at the Wynn. Except for Johanna, Roge, Skyler, Misty, Gordo, and Skone who walked to the lobby bar and ordered a few shots. Roge insisted they hop on some Birds and scoot to Cheetah's Night Club. As an ex-porn star, Roge still had a few connections in Vegas and was able to reserve a table at center stage.

Roge ordered another round for the yogis. "I'm telling you, you have to flex with the yoga rules. Take your shirt off, teach with a thong. Maybe do a little body-to-body adjustment in Dog. You guys are all smoking hot. Sex yoga up!"

Gordo screamed, "Hey, Roge! How about we put stripper poles in the yoga room?"

Roge smiled and said, "Already did, brother! Students love it!"

"And allow cell phones and selfies in class."

"I do that, too!" Roge looked to Misty. "Misty, I love the Netflix idea. Imagine students being able to practice yoga while they binge-watch their favorite show. Super spiritual."

"Yeah, I mean why should students have to miss their favorite TV show just to fit in some yoga."

"Cheers to cell phones and Netflix in the yoga studio!"

Everyone raised a shot glass and shouted, "CHEERS!"

Johanna took a sip and added,. "I haven't told anyone but last week I started to post IG stories when I teach. I tagged a few students. They told me it made them feel spiritual."

Misty piped in. "I started taking Savasana pics of my students. Looks super spiritual on IG."

"Exactly. No one gives a fuck!"

The lights went out, the music pumped even louder as the crowd went berserk. THE MC got on the mic....

"Ladies and gentlemen. The main event! Give A WARM Cheetah's welcome to Carly and Asia!"

Billowing smoke from fog machines enveloped the stage, adding to the electric energy. As the smoke dissipated and the strobe lights turned on, a silhouette of Asia and Carly's long, perfectly toned bodies appeared on stage. Wearing tight mesh see-through tank tops, black stilettos, and tiny black G-strings, Asia and Carly moved in X-rated unison as "Erotic City" blasted through the sound system. With their tongues darting in and out, Asia and Carly seductively slithered, twisted, and coiled around each other. Entwined in every feasible direction, they took turns pouring massage oil over their already slick bodies. Then, ever so slowly, in unison, Asia and Carly placed their fingers between their lips. While still pressed against each other, they teasingly raised their tank tops over their heads and embraced into a prolonged erotic french kiss. The crowd exploded into an orgasmic frenzy, transfixed by their goddess-like aura.

Roge couldn't help himself and turned to Gordo. "Hey Gordo, I bet you're feeling spiritual now."

"WELCOME TO VEGAS, SKYLER!"

"This is so fucking spiritual."

"Sexy and spiritual as fuck!"

Asia and Carly were only getting started. Placing her hands on the floor, Asia inched her stilettos up the pole. Like a trapeze artist, she slowly released her feet away and positioned her body into a gravity-defying Handstand. With a seductive look, she bent her knees, arched her back, and curled her spine towards a hypnotic version of Scorpion Pose.

Roge yelled out, "Hey, that's a yoga pose! It's like Stripper Scorpion!"

Meanwhile, just a few feet away, Carly was performing her own yoga strip show. Dropping to her knees and spreading her legs wide, Carly slowly arched her back into a topless variation of Camel Pose. Twisting her body even further, she swung her legs out in front for a naughty variation of Dandasana. Gordo couldn't hold back. "They're doing yoga! That's a Forward Fold!" Roge hurled a hundred-dollar bill on stage, yelling, "A Stripper Forward Fold!"

From her Forward Fold, Carly effortlessly contorted her back, lifted her body, and transitioned from Upward Facing Dog to Down Dog completing a *Sexy Vinyasa*. As Carly held Dog, Asia inched closer and circled her like a tigress stalking its prey. Stopping directly behind Carly, Asia raised her hand high in the air, egging and waving the crowd on. On the count of three, Asia's hand whipped downwards and landed directly on Carly's glistening, taut buttocks. SMACK!

Twenties, fifties, and hundred dollar bills were piling up across the stage. And then… Another SMACK! Like a smack heard 'round the world, Carly and Asia performed a wild and spiritual incarnation of Down Dog Spank Pose. But they STILL weren't done. Planting her hands on Carly's back, Asia then lifted her legs into the air, holding Handstand directly on top of Carly. Johanna, Roge, Skyler, Gordo, Misty, and Skone couldn't believe their eyes as they witnessed some pseudo-sexual version of yoga never seen before.

Misty yelled out, "I think they're doing yoga."

Roge agreed. "That's totally yoga. My students would freak out over them."

"It's sexy as fuck!"

"Totally spiritual!"

Gordo grabbed his phone, opened up Instagram, did a quick search, and found Asia. Her bio read:

"Dancer, Lover of Life and Yogi."

"Guys, she's a yogi!"

Misty didn't believe it. "Yeah, right Gordo."

"I'm serious. Her Instagram says she teaches here in Vegas and she has 450,000 followers!"

Misty looked up Carly on IG. "Carly's a yogi, too! Dancer, Yogi and Spiritual AF."

With his eyes still fixed on Carly and Asia, Skone said, "I'd totally go to one of their classes."

Roge put his arm around Skone. "Dude, the whole fucking state of California would go to their classes! We have to get them to do a workshop in LA."

Carly and Asia made their way to center stage and like two synchronized swimmers, bent their knees and elbows and simultaneously lifted up into Stripper Crow Pose. They effortlessly lifted their legs away from their forearms, straightened their legs to the sky, and took one final version of Stripper Handstand.

Howls, screams, and whistling continued to pierce the air as the lights went out. The spiritually charged yoga strip show officially came to an end. Johanna and the group of yogis jumped to their feet and gave a standing O.

Roge whistled and cheered. "I feel so spiritual. That is what I'm talking about, people!"

Skone, an ex-gymnast turned yoga teacher shouted, "That was the best yoga class ever! All that upside-down gymnastics stuff is super spiritual."

Misty couldn't believe what she was hearing from her yogi friends.

"Stop. THAT was not yoga. They're strippers. WE ARE IN A STRIP CLUB!"

"Hello… That was Down Dog! And Crow Pose!"

"In a thong, Roge! We don't do yoga in a thong!"

"Hey, you were the one who suggested Netflix in class!"

"Yes, but not strippers!"

"Come on, all of that was yoga. Down Dog, Up Dog, I saw a little Malasana in there, too."

"You saw ASS, Roge!"

"That was freaking yoga. Don't you feel more spiritual after watching that?"

"Aroused — maybe. Spiritual — no."

"It's the same thing!"

Johanna was still cheering and squeezed in a few strip club selfies. "They were incredible! I want them to teach me Crow in a thong! Roge, we have to bring them to Santa Monica! We should open a studio!"

Roge's brain was working overtime. "Guys, Jo's right! That's yoga! We allow cell phones, selfies in class, loud music. Make class feel like a dance club. Or a strip show."

Gordo agreed. "Dude, love it! I'm in."

Misty still wasn't buying it.

"Roge, you're insane. What would Buddha say? This is crazy."

"Buddha would love this stuff!"

"Yoga isn't about getting nude and crude, Roge."

"No one knows what the fuck yoga is! We pop all this shit on Instagram and give it some yoga hashtags. BAM, it's yoga! Can you all do Handstand?"

Everyone nodded.

"Then we're golden. This is yoga!"

Skyler still wasn't sold on the idea. "Roge, you're buzzed on tequila. You can't be serious?"

"Fuck yeah, I'm serious. Ever since I started wearing a thong, my students tell me how much more spiritual I make them feel. My classes are jammed."

Johanna jumped in and said, "He's right, Sky. There's a line to get in."

Roge continued. "Everyone keeps complaining about class sizes dropping. So fucking let's use Instagram in yoga class. Allow Netflix. Encourage more selfies. What are we doing wasting time on the breath? Why do yogis care so much about the breath? Look at me. I'm breathing! And when I'm dead, I'm not breathing!"

Misty still wasn't sure.

"Roge, NO ONE is going to go for it."

"Misty, you keep saying no one is showing up to your classes. Take selfies. Throw on a bikini. Rub some oil on your body before class. Be creative!"

"But what about the sutras?"

Roge leaned in close. "People don't give a fuck about SUTRAS!"

Johanna looked re-energized and inspired by the back and forth. "Roge is right. We all have six-packs, we all look fucking hot, and we can hold Handstand!"

Misty still wasn't sold and yelled back, "HANDSTAND ISN'T YOGA, JO!"

Roge placed his hands on Misty's shoulders. "Misty, listen to me. Everything is yoga. This strip club is yoga."

"It's not yoga, Roge. It's gymnastics, tits, and ass."

"I'm telling you. This is yoga! A hot ass is yoga. Handstand is freaking yoga. Look at how spiritual everyone looks. Come on, who's with me?"

Everyone raised their shot glass. Everyone except Misty.

"Guys, listen to me! Yoga isn't about looking hot on Instagram!"

Roge was losing his patience. "Misty, just slap some stupid Rumi quote underneath a hot pic of your ass, and BAM, that's yoga!"

The following day, everyone reconvened at the Holiday Inn free breakfast buffet, and still, the issues were the same.

Roge pleaded with the group. "How about at least a selfie during Savasana? I'm telling you, it's super-spiritual. And one group selfie after class. Students love it."

Sipping on her lukewarm coffee, Ashwala said, "You want students to take selfies and wear thongs. I can't listen to this. Roge, you are a disgrace to yoga."

"I'm trying to fix yoga!"

Chewing on a stale croissant, Vishypu mumbled, "Roge, maybe YOU have to dive deeper into YOUR practice, go on a Vipassana and reconnect with your yoga."

"Maybe YOU need to get a clue, Vishy. People want followers. They want to look hot. That's it. That's yoga. Instagram doesn't care about Vipass or whatever the hell you call it."

The group of yogis had just about reached the end of Day Two when Roge received a text.

Jumping up and running to the door, he shouted, "They're here! They're here!"

Misty asked, "Who's here?"

Walking back inside, Roge was flanked by Asia and Carly.

"Everyone, meet Asia and Carly. Asia and Carly, say hello. We met last night at Cheetah's."

Victoria, studio owner of Lakhti Hakhti from New York, had been quiet most of the weekend. Sneering at Roge, she finally spoke up. "So while all of us true yogis take in a sound bath, you get a lap dance at Cheetah's."

"Vicki, it was very spiritual, and I went with Johanna, Skyler, Misty, Gordo, and Skone. And Carly and Asia aren't just dancers; they're yogis, just like you and me. Instagram famous yogis."

"Ha, I don't believe it."

"They've both completed 200-hour training, teach here in Vegas, and have 400,000 followers! Vicki, how many followers do you have?!"

"I don't use Instagram, Roge!"

"That explains why your classes are so lame, Vickster!"

Johanna could sense tempers were rising. Hoping to defuse the tension, she dimmed the lights and turned on Madonna's "Vogue".

"Everyone, Asia and Carly are going to demo this sexy new style of yoga. We don't have a name for it yet, but we think this is cutting edge. It's very similar to what Roge is doing in his class."

Roge added, "The future of yoga."

Asia and Carly ripped off their jackets, revealing the same outfits as last night. Asia pulled out a bottle of baby oil and massaged oil over Carly's body.

Roge walked to the front of the room, "Ladies, show us your Hot Sexy Warrior Two."

Asia and Carly bent their front thigh, stretched their arms wide, and held Warrior Two.

"Now show us Triangle and Warrior One Thong Pose."

With the room's rapt attention, Asia and Carly deftly moved through the classical yoga standing postures and added the A and B flow series. Roge grabbed his phone and took some pics. "Amazing, ladies! Let's spice it up. Show everyone the Down Dog Spank Pose. Super spiritual. I think I'm going to have to try that in my class."

Asia made her way to Downward Facing Dog, and as she pressed her buttocks towards the air, Carly walked over and smacked her right across her flexed butt cheeks. Groans were heard from the traditional yogis.

"Are you serious, Roge?"

With that, at least half of the attendees grabbed their mats and left. "Roge, you're a pig. All of you are disgusting!"

Roge ignored them and continued to frantically take more pics.

"It's okay, ladies. Their studios will be closed in a few months. They don't know what true yoga is anymore."

More yogis grabbed their mats and exited the yoga dance party.

"Do that Crow into Handstand thing!"

Johanna turned the music up even louder. "Let's see Handstand!"

"Handstand isn't yoga, Jo!"

Johanna yelled back, "IT IS NOW!"

From Handstand, Carly and Asia magically lifted one hand off the ground and held One-Handed Handstand.

Skone's mouth dropped open. "What the fuck is that?"

Carly was still upside down. "It's One-Handed Handstand. It's super hot on the Gram. All my stories this week are One-Handed."

Johanna turned to Roge. "Roge, post some of these on Instagram."

"On it, Jo!"

Rebecca, who was born on an ashram and owned retreat centers throughout Hawai'i and California, had seen enough.

"All of you should be banned from the Alliance. What are you doing to my beloved practice? THIS ISNT YOGA! They are erotic dancers. They probably don't know anything about the Sutras."

Roge yelled back, "No one cares about Sutras!"

"I have spent my life devoted to the Sutras. I'm trying to pass this knowledge on to my students. To enrich people's lives. The Sutras are everything to yoga."

Roge yelled, "Hey Asia, go hold Warrior Two! And Carly, give Asia a big Sutra spank!"

Rebecca grabbed her mala beads, her organic yoga mat and tromped towards the door. Vishypu, Ashwala, and the last few remaining yogis from the conference grabbed their yoga mats and also exited in disgust. Rebecca turned her head and, with one last parting shot, "I will not subject myself to this nauseating display. This isn't yoga, and it never will be. Instagram isn't yoga. Go to India and reconnect with your bandhas."

Roge responded with a wicked smile and added, "Hey, Asia! Go smack Carly on her bandhas!"

The door slammed shut. Roge looked at his phone with a giant smile.

"The Handstand shot of Asia has 2,000 likes! The Warrior Two Spank has 5,000! And look at all the Heart emojis! I feel so spiritual!"

"What hashtags did you use?"

"#Yoga, #Handstand, #thong, #sexyyoga, and #stripperpole."

"Did anyone report you or say it isn't yoga?"

"Oh, come on. Who is going to report me? I keep telling you, if you hashtag yoga, it's fucking yoga!"

With some concern, Skone walked over to Roge. "Dude, love the energy, but you heard everyone. It sure as hell looks like strippers and gymnastics. We're kind of making yoga all about sex."

"Bro, what about last night? You were totally into this. We all agreed this has to be yoga."

"Look, last night was spiritual as fuck, but everyone left. Dude, no one is here."

"I'm here. Jo's here. Gordo and Skyler, and Misty are here. Carly and Asia! Skone, I need you, brother. This is the only way yoga is ever going to work. Are you guys with me or what?"

Asia, Carly, and the whole group of yogis wrapped their arms around Roge and gave him a group hug.

"We're with you, Roge."

Everyone raised their phones in the air.

Engulfed by the group of sexy yogis, Roge yelled out, "Instagram, say hello to the Spiritual Eight! It's time to make yoga feel sexy and spiritual as fuck!"

Over the next twenty-four hours, Roge, Carly, Asia, and the rest of the group worked to revolutionize yoga and create a more refined version of sexual spirituality.

Skone looked to Roge for guidance, "Roge, what's the plan? What do we do first? Call India?"

"What the fuck? No way, dude."

"How about the Yoga Alliance?"

"Stop it! Sexy yoga has nothing to do with India or the Yoga freaking Alliance. We have to figure out which poses look the hottest and inspire people to take their clothes off and post selfies. Postures that look boring, we drop. Postures that look hot, we keep."

Johanna yelled out, "Handstand!"

"Yes. Definitely. Anything upside down is in."

"Scorpion!"

"Totally!"

Everyone formed a semi-circle and threw out ideas.

"No Savasana! And no Child's Pose!"

"Yes, exactly!"

"No Happy Baby!"

"Happy baby, stretches, Savasana, Restorative Postures, ALL OUT!"

Skyler grabbed a pen and started making a list.

"No Child's Pose? You sure? It's kind of an important pose, Roge."

"Not anymore. Child's Pose is over!"

"Can we at least suggest a Child's Pose?"

"NO! And if anyone takes a Child's Pose, you kick them out of class."

"Okay, so no Child's Pose, no Happy Baby, or any relaxing or stretchy pose."

"Exactly."

Asia leaned in towards Roge.

"Carly and I had this idea where we take selfies while we hold postures. Demo it, Carly."

Carly grabbed her phone and selfie stick, held Warrior Two, and snapped a bunch of selfies. She stepped up into Half Moon and took Half Moon selfies and then went through an entire sequence taking selfies in each posture.

Roge rushed to Asia and Carly and gave them a high-five. "Why the fuck didn't I think of this? It's spiritual and sexy. Genius!"

Skone asked, "Can either of you take a selfie in Handstand?"

Asia raised her hand. "I can. So can Carly! And we have a workshop every week on Handstand and Selfie Handstands!"

Skyler went back to taking notes. "So maybe we say like Handstand is the most spiritual pose. We do Handstand on rocks. Handstand on our cars. At the airport. In the elevator. On bridges. At the grocery store. On the side of buildings. We do Handstand everywhere."

Misty asked, "And post them on Instagram?"

"Yes, DUH!"

Roge looked to Johanna. "Get Melo on the phone. We need some of these yoga apparel companies to jump on this. Gordo, aren't you friends with someone at Spiritual Mofo?"

Gordo grabbed his phone. "They'd totally be into this. Texting them now!"

Something was still bothering Misty. She looked nervous when she spoke. "Um… Guys, um… I'm sorry. I have to tell you something."

"What is it?"

"I feel pathetic."

"Tell us, Misty."

After a pause she blurted out, "I can't do Handstand! I know, it's lame, but I can't do it."

"You said last night…"

"I know what I said, but I lied, ok?"

"Seriously?"

"Seriously. I can't do it!"

"Not even against the wall?"

"I get too scared. What do I do? If I can't hold Handstand, I won't get as many followers, and then I won't be spiritual. I'm screwed, right?"

Roge walked over and took Misty's hand.

"Well you don't need to hold Handstand when you have jugs like these, Misty! Perfect for yoga, and they're super spiritual!"

Misty couldn't help but blush.

"Stop it."

"Misty, your chest is freaking spiritual as fuck. Every Insta pic you post is about your gorgeous knockers. No breath, just breasts. And do every posture in a bikini. Bikini Standing Postures or Topless Yoga with the nipples X'd out. Hashtag #boobyoga or #toplessyoga. Your Insta will freaking explode. Everything is yoga, Misty!"

The look on Misty's face changed from doubt to inspiration. "And maybe I wear a thong when I teach?"

"ABSOLUTELY! And carry a yoga strap and whip people in Down Dog."

Carly blurted out, "I do that! My students love it!"

Roge looked to Misty reassuringly and said, "See?"

"You know guys… I think I can do that."

Skone piped in with another suggestion.

"I have it, Misty. How 'bout you do yoga in the shower. Call it Shower Yoga. Video cameras all around you. Water all over your body. Steam everywhere. That is your yoga."

"Thanks guys. I feel so much better. I'll do both. Shower AND Bikini Yoga!"

Roge added, "We can have like Shower Yoga workshops. Maybe even Bathtub Yoga. Teach people how to hold postures and take selfies in the shower. So spiritual!"

After a few moments, Johanna walked back in, grinning from ear to ear.

"I got through to Melo. They're in!"

The Spiritual Eight jumped up and shrieked with enthusiasm.

"They said they're totally into it. They've been wanting to do this, but they were too worried the yoga community would black-ball them. They'll redo their marketing and make it about sex, looking skinny and hot, and Handstand. They'll tag all of us!"

Gordo's phone buzzed with a text from Spiritual Mofo.

"Spiritual Mofo is in, too!"

Johanna hopped into Handstand. "Roge, take a pic of me! Quick! I want to see how many likes I get!"

Skone went back to looking at his notes and talking to himself.

"So I post non-stop Handstand pics. Wear a tight Speedo and post on Instagram as much as I can. Just making sure I have it right."

"Yes," Roge said. "And this is really important. When we hire teachers, they should have at least 20,000 followers. Minimum. If their Instagram sucks, then they're useless. Hire teachers who have a background in gymnastics. Ex-models, actors, pole dancers. Anyone who's comfortable in front of a camera. And you implement a dress code in class. Everyone's in a thong, bikini, or Speedo. No exceptions."

Carly raised her hand. "We like to hand out free thongs and Speedos to all new members. It builds a sense of community."

Roge loved the flow of ideas. "If we spend the next six months committed to this and hashtag #yoga, #Handstand, #sex, #naked, #spiritual..."

Skyler yelled out, "How about #yogaeverydamnday?!"

"YES, LOVE THAT! YOGA EVERY DAMN DAY!"

The spiritual inspiration continued until the wee hours of the morning as The Spiritual Eight created the freshest, most innovative, and spiritual type of yoga ever imaginable. With Asia and Carly's background in pole dancing, Skone's background in gymnastics, Gordo's hot abs, Misty's voluptuous breasts, Skyler and Jo's modeling background, and Roge's experience in porn, they had all the elements needed to bring SSAFY to life.

"Hey Roge, let's say students can't hold Handstand like Misty?"

"Then abs. Nothing but core. Yoga bicycles. Forearm plank. Do like ab giveaways. Ab contests. Whoever has the best ab selfie in class wins a prize. And Gordo, you should be the ab guru. Your abs are insane. Change all of your classes to ab classes!"

Gordo smiled and raised his shirt.

Roge put his face next to Gordo's abs and took a selfie. "I mean look at these things!"

Gordo grabbed a bottle of baby oil and rubbed oil all over his belly. "I should take like 100 ab selfies a day."

Roge yelled out, "No way! Five hundred ab selfies a day! And let students take selfies with your abs. Your Insta will go nuts!"

Jo had another suggestion. "We do weekly Handstand workshops and ab workshops!"

Skyler yelled out, "Selfie and belfie workshops!"

Misty piped in. "What do we call this, Roge?"

"Sex yoga?"

"Hot sexy yoga?"

"How 'bout hot yoga?"

"Yoga sweat?"

"Sweat as fuck yoga?"

"Stripper yoga!"

"Porn yoga!"

Asia stood up. "What do you think of SSAFY?"

Roge looked intrigued. "What's that stand for?"

"Sexy Spiritual As Fuck Yoga."

Roge took a moment to let the name soak in and said, "I love it! SSAFY! That's it! I'm feeling it, guys! And we hand out selfie sticks and take group selfies at the end of class instead of Savasana. We put a TV screen inside the studio with everyone's Instagram."

Johanna had a proud smile on her face. "Roge, it's perfect. You're like a Sexy Swami."

"Sexy Spiritual As Fuck Yoga is officially going to save yoga!"

Everyone cheered, gave high-fives, and took a few more rounds of selfies, but Roge wasn't finished.

"Guys, I have a surprise. BIG news. One of my investors from the porn world wants in! I texted him last night. I was feeling spiritually inspired. We have the perfect spot. In Santa Monica. Seven blocks from the beach. Home of the first SSAFY studio, and I want each of you to come work with me. Give me six months, and I guarantee we will all be IG yoga superstars. We'll be the most spiritual yoga teachers in the world. Hundreds of sponsors. Millions of followers. Are you with me or what?!"

Misty, Carly, Skone, and the rest of the Spiritual Eight leaped in the air and responded with an emphatic "YES!"

Johanna grabbed her phone. "Group selfie time!"

Roge yelled out, "Everyone, strip down to your underwear and hop into Handstand. Misty, take off your top. We'll hold Handstand, you just stand there and do Topless Crescent. Amazing work today, sexy yogis. Time to introduce Instagram to SSAFY!"

CHAPTER 7
The Future of Yoga

Even before Vegas, Roge was already toying with some of the SSAFY elements, but with his very own studio in the works, Roge was prepared to create the most sexually spiritual yoga classes the world had ever seen. One night, while watching his vast library of old DVDs, Roge had one of those "AH-HA moments." What about a Yoga Porn channel to complement the spirituality of the SSAFY studio?

Roge reconnected with old industry friends and worked on setting up his own yoga studio inside his five-bedroom Benedict Canyon home. He put yoga mats in the bedrooms, by the pool, next to the hot tub, and within a week, he had a full-time production crew with some of the porn industry's finest writers, directors, and actors. A month later, he not only opened the doors to SSAFY Santa Monica but launched the first-ever Yoga Porn Channel. Roge's channel captured a spontaneity never felt before in yoga. One second he was holding Warrior One. The next moment he felt a strong spiritual urge to rip off his Speedo, walk onto his student's mat, slowly undress them and engage in

Warrior One sex. Sometimes he got the spiritual urges in Down Dog. The next day, Warrior Two or Crescent Pose could be Roge's source for inspiration. Back and forth he went, yoga-then-sex-sex-then yoga, making each class his own unique spiritual journey. To top it off, instead of Savasana, Roge ended each YouTube class by engaging in five minutes of french kissing or heavy petting with one lucky student.

As for his Instagram, Roge created his own personal SSAFY algorithm; a custom-made formula guaranteeing the most likes, emojis, comments, followers, and spiritual engagement. Twenty-five percent of his posts were still-shots taken directly from his Yoga Porn Channel. Action shots, body shots, lip and muscle pics. Roge became a master of side-angle ass, crotch, and nipple selfies, ensuring his porn stills would always pass through IG censors. Having been blessed with long, thick flowing black hair, Roge devotes another twenty-five percent of his IG to hair selfies. Comb-your-hair-selfies, color-the-grey selfies, tie-your-hair-up-in-a-bun selfies, and wash-your-hair selfies. Another fifteen percent of his Instagram pics include electric bike and skateboard selfies. *I wonder what Roge does with the other thirty-five percent of his Instagram algorithm?*

With all the attention from his yoga channel and his innovative daily selfies, Roge's studio classes became a smashing success. Classes sold out weeks in advance. Lines formed down the street and around the courtyard, with students eager to learn the ins and outs of SSAFY. He created a special VIP section reserved only for students who could hold Handstand. He included perks for students with a sexy six-pack; free alkaline water ice baths, SSAFY loofah sponges and SSAFY certified organic almond milk. He took Carly's advice and handed out thongs and Speedos to all new members. He installed a bar inside the studio so students could grab a quick refreshing cocktail or green juice while they flowed. Roge hired top Vegas DJs and guaranteed each student at least three Down Dog spanks per class. He installed cameras in the showers for those infamous shower selfies, and to top it off, students were also guaranteed a pre and post-class selfie with Roge.

Despite the success and free-spirit nature of his public classes, Roge was sensible enough to know yoga wasn't quite the same as pornography. Yoga still had traditions and rules, and as much as he wanted to, Roge knew he couldn't teach class in the nude. Still, Roge wanted to do whatever he could to create as sexually spiritual an environment as possible. To achieve that goal without taking off ALL of his clothes, Roge made the executive choice to teach his classes wearing only a Speedo or a tight-fitting thong.

Students came to appreciate the bird's eye view of Roge's privates while they flowed, and pretty soon, the front row became known as "the most spiritual place on earth." When the doors opened, students flocked to claim their spot upfront to feel that extra dash of spirituality. With his thong or Speedo wrapped snugly around his crotch, students often just stood and stared. Students were transfixed, and the tighter and skimpier the fit, the more students couldn't keep their eyes away. Feeling the growing aura and popularity of his testes, Roge believed there was no better way to give back to the community than to devote the final thirty-five percent of his profile to... *Thong selfies?* Not just thong selfies. Testicle selfies.

Roge was always vain about his good looks, but he was by far the proudest of his man berries. Perfectly round and perfectly sized, Roge's package went on to become the most recognizable set of nuts in the entire yoga community. Whether shining a spotlight on them in class or sharing them in his daily thong selfies, Roge ensures the outline of his spiritual sac is always prominent. Roge became a thong-and-testicle selfie master and went on to create weekly Private Part Selfie Workshops and instructional videos. Suffice to say, his students couldn't get enough. Be on the lookout for the @rogeshotspiritualballs page to land on Instagram by the end of the year.

After the Vegas weekend, Misty was convinced that the only path to a thriving IG following was to implement Skone's suggestion… Boob and Shower Yoga. Despite her lifelong insecurities, Misty had always known that her breasts were her greatest feature, and she was prepared to do whatever she could to flaunt them for SSAFY. Misty already had a vast collection of bikinis and tight, low-cut tanks, but to bring Boob and Shower Yoga to life, her moldy, pink-tiled, 4 ft. by 4 ft. fifties-style bathroom needed a major upgrade.

After speaking to multiple designers, the only solution was to ditch the kitchen, knock a wall down and turn her 250 square-foot Venice bungalow into a sleek, open, and modern style bathroom. With soothing grey and white tones, granite countertops, stone flooring, and wall-to-wall mirrors, it became the perfect spiritual backdrop for Shower Yoga. Her bathroom had it all—spa jets, double rain showers, custom dimmable lighting, candles, and potpourri in every corner. A freestanding

6-foot soaking tub as well as video cameras on the walls and showerheads to capture erotic shower and bathtub selfies from every feasible angle.

Misty went on to develop one-of-a-kind instructional videos teaching students how to safely take selfies and practice yoga while showering. She also created a Forward Fold series teaching students how to capture selfies in a bathtub while holding a Forward Fold. Her underwater bathtub series was especially a hit, with followers eager to learn how to take sexy selfies while underwater.

She posts a Live Instagram feed from her bathtub every evening, inviting her followers to share a glass of wine during her nightly bathtub meditation. Her Instagram has grown past 500,000 followers, and her Shower Yoga instructional videos have set records in the fitness industry. She is currently the only SSAFY instructor certified in Shower Yoga, and when she's not in the studio, she is traveling around the world designing in-home Shower Yoga studios for clients.

Even from a young age, Skone was drawn to living a life upside down. He loved hanging from the jungle gym at school, from his top bunk-bed at home, and out his bedroom window. He even liked to watch his favorite cartoon, Spiderman, upside down. Skone tried his very first Handstand at the age of ten, and he's been holding them #everydamnday since.

After Vegas, Skone was crowned the official SSAFY Handstand guru, and turned all of his classes into Handstand workshops. Skone posts over 100 Handstand selfies and stories a day and is committed to helping all SSAFY members flip upside down within the first month of their membership. When Skone isn't at the SSAFY studio, you can find him at some of his favorite local hangouts working on new variations of his favorite posture: at the Venice Beach post office, in the produce aisle at Erewhon, on the balcony of his apartment, on the Venice Canal Bridge or with his dog, Kryo.

Be sure to check out the SSAFY wesbite and IG page and sign up for one of Skone's upcoming spiritual workshops:

- Waterfall Handstand

- Escalator Handstand

- Alligator Handstand

- Basketball Handstand

- Sushi Handstand

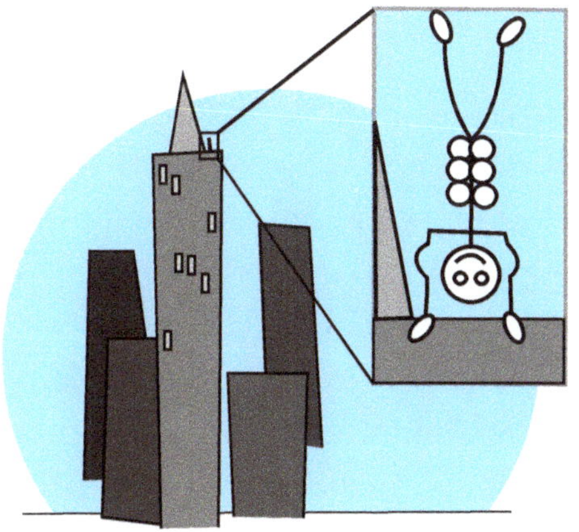

Jo had the foresight to realize SSAFY isn't just about yoga; it's a complete lifestyle. It's a "brand." Yoga should be the food you eat, the juice you drink, how you style your hair, the clothes you wear, where you buy your shoes, and where you take happy-hour selfies. Jo installed 4K video cameras in her car, creating the perfect environment for daily inspirational car selfies. Jo then installed cameras throughout her 800 square-foot Venice Beach apartment and created daily yoga flows for her adoring fans and followers. Favorites include The Good Morning Granola Flow, the Five-Minute Coffee Flow, and the Afternoon Pedicure Flow, where she holds postures while giving herself a Diva pedicure. For her Youtube channel, Jo created the Evening Lingerie Yoga Flow, recording nightly time-lapse videos as she flows in silk lingerie. For those who want to keep up with her two pets, Shanaya and Wonton, Jo created the Thong Puppy Flow and the Thong Kitty Cat Flow.

Jo created a vast array of inspirational selfies for Instagram. Shave your legs selfies and shop for shoes selfies. Side-angle ass selfies, the mimosa and cacao smoothie selfie, the massage selfie, the walk your dog and drink organic wine selfie, the spray your face with a refreshing elixir selfie, the toes in the sand selfie, and the farmer's market eat an organic apple selfie. Jo came up with the Sunday sunrise beach bikini women's-only meditation circle where yoginis sit in a circle and take bikini selfies while meditating. In an interview for *Yoga Ab Magazine*, Jo was asked about her intention on Instagram. "It's all about LOVE. I want my followers to LOVE me as much as I LOVE myself."

Johanna even went on to create an Instagram mentorship program. For the cost of $10,000, she teaches students how to fully integrate SSAFY and Instagram into every aspect of their lives. Jo's spiritual butt cheeks have been "liked" more often than any other set of cheeks in the SSAFY community. She also set the IG story world record by posting 338 IG stories in a single day. Johanna hasn't taught an actual yoga class in over two years, yet she is regarded as one of the most sexual and spiritual yoga teachers in the entire SSAFY community.

As for the final two members of the Spiritual Eight, after the Vegas convention, Carly and Asia packed up their lingerie, bikinis, cut-off shorts and their yoga strip show paraphernalia, drove to Los Angeles, and joined Roge to become the most popular and sexually spiritual yoga teachers in the world.

CHAPTER 8
my sexually spiritual yoga High

I took Roge's suggestion and opted for a few shower selfies. I tried on my brand new Speedo, squirted the SSAFY shower gel on my body, and smiled at the cameras. As I stood there, basking in the joy of my first shower selfie, my mind wandered back towards Ashwala and The Yoga Sanctuary. I couldn't help but wonder if it was time to quit my old studio and officially join SSAFY. The Sanctuary never made me feel this connected to my yoga practice. There were no group selfies at the Sanctuary. Ashwala never handed me a Speedo or a selfie stick. The Sanctuary showers didn't have cameras installed for shower selfies. No one at the Sanctuary ever talked about getting spanked, and Roge seemed much more spiritual than Vishypu.

Everything I ever knew about yoga felt like a complete lie, and at that moment, while I took my tenth post-class shower selfie, I realized it was time to start my practice all over again. Thanks to Roge, Carly, and Asia, I felt a newfound sense of spiritual inspiration, and I was convinced SSAFY was the perfect place to recharge my yoga practice. I stepped out of the shower, and as I prepared to post my first ever shower selfie, I was 100 percent convinced I was ready to become a sexy yogi.

I ran out of the locker room. Asia was toweling off behind the front desk.

"Asia, I posted my shower selfie!"

"Oh, super hot. Did you tag SSAFY?!"

"YEP!"

"I'll totally like it and share it."

"Where's Roge? I wanna show him."

"Roge has a Feather Flow class going on."

"Well, sign me up, Asia! I can't believe how spiritual I feel. This place is great!"

Asia beamed at me.

"Yay, I was hoping you'd join today. Your Instagram already looks better. You're going to be at 10,000 followers by the end of the week. I promise."

"I'm ready for SSAFY!"

"You're totally ready. I just need you to sign our contract and a waiver. While you fill that out, I'll get your SSAFY selfie stick. You get a goodie bag, too!"

"Thanks, Asia!" *What about Ashwala!? What the hell are you doing!? What about Vishypu?! You can't seriously be joining this place! Yes-yes-yes! I'm joining! Asia says I'll be at 10,000 followers! This isn't yoga! Yes it is! I feel so spiritual!*

With yogis and yoginis everywhere, tanning on the sundeck, drinking green juice, and staring at their phones while taking selfies, SSAFY felt like a true community. Everyone looked so spiritual, and as I gazed at the roomful of sexy yogis, and stared at the naked black and white photos of Carly and Asia on the walls, I had never felt so confident I was making the right decision.

With my membership, I received a goodie bag filled with two brand new pink Speedos, three bottles of green juice, a coupon for a free wheatgrass shot, and a brand new selfie stick. Asia handed me an SSAFY handbook and a few hand-outs to help me familiarize myself with SSAFY. There was a brochure that explained the history of SSAFY. One about what it means to live the life of a sexy yogi. Booklets about SSAFY philosophy and the various Selfie Standing Postures. There was a brochure listing all the sexy certified restaurants, cafes, and juice shops that offered discounts to SSAFY members. There was a brochure about upcoming SSAFY workshops. Workshops on Handstands and selfies and Instagram filters. A workshop about how to get six-pack abs within a month. Workshops about beach and sunset selfies. A one-week intensive exploring belfies and Instagram. There was an upcoming retreat in Bali teaching sexy yogis how to take selfies in front of a waterfall. Carly was even hosting a retreat in Tulum that promised all attendees 3,000 new followers and an extra 10,000 follower bonus to yogis who can hold Dining-Table Handstand at Hartstone.

The critical voices screamed at me. *STOP! What are you doing?! You can't join this place! This place isn't yoga! This place is a freak show!* But when I looked at my signature on the dotted line, I knew I was making the right choice, and my life would never be the same. I tossed my ratty shorts into the trash, turned to Asia and Carly, and asked if we could take one more group selfie.

"Thanks again, Carly and Asia. This place is so spiritual. I'll see you tomorrow!"

"Look for a "Welcome to SSAFY" DM tonight. And FYI, this week, we have a bunch of workshops you have to check out. Belfies, filters, and Skone's workshop on Handstands."

"Can't wait!"

I grabbed my mat and goodie-bag and turned to leave when Carly placed her hands on my shoulders.

"Hold on, Eddie. One more thing."

"A good-bye selfie?"

"You have to quit your old yoga studio. You've outgrown that place."

"Oh, right. The Sanctuary?"

"Yuck. That place is old news. You have to get out of there."

"You're positive I'm ready for SSAFY?"

"Definitely. Run over there and get out of that contract, and we'll see you and your sexy Speedos tomorrow."

Despite some initial trepidation, deep down, I knew Carly and Asia were right. I had to quit my old studio and close the chapter on my past yoga life. *I can't believe you're leaving the Sanctuary!*

You love that place. Your practice has grown so much thanks to Vishypu and your breath is strong. Fuck that place, Eddie! No one cares about breathing! That place has wasted years of your life. They never told you about selfies, thongs, bikinis. No keg stands. Drop 'em!

I parked my Bird and ran inside, where I was met with a smattering of Namastes. *How many times do they have to say Namaste?! What did Roge say? NO MORE NAMASTES!*

Ashwala was behind the desk, checking people into class.

"Hi, Ashwala." *Apologize, you idiot! You flaked on your date! She's going to hate you. Show her your shower selfie!*

"Namaste, Eddie." *Ugh. Another freaking Namaste.*

"I'm sorry about dinner the other night."

"Don't worry about it. There's a sound bath tonight. You wanna go?"

"Yeah, not sure about a sound bath. I kind of want to talk about my membership." *I can't do this. Yes, you can! No, I can't! YOU HAVE TO! Quit this ridiculous place, NOW!*

Ashwala bowed her head and whispered another "Namaste." She clearly didn't hear me.

"I think it's time I cancel my membership to the studio."

"Om, Shanti."

"Ashwala. Please, listen to me."

"Ommmmmmmmmmmm."

AHHHHHHHHHH!! Why isn't she listening?

I grabbed Ashwala's hands.

"Ashwala. I don't want to practice here anymore. I'd like to end my membership as of today."

"Of course. We can put your membership on hold. Have you signed up for the month-long retreat to India? So many of our students are going."

"No, I'm not going to India. Please, Ashwala. I just want to end my contract."

"You sure? Vishy and I were just noticing how your practice is really starting to grow. Your breath has sounded strong. Why don't we try a cleansing breath together?"

"You're not hearing me. I don't care about the breath anymore."

"The breath is a vital component to the practice."

"Please, can I just quit the Yoga Sanctuary?"

"I don't understand."

"You never taught me selfies. No Instagram. No one here takes Handstand selfies."

"Eddie, you aren't making any sense. What's going on with you?"

"Does Vishypu even know how to take Handstand?"

"Handstand?"

"And what about shower selfies? You guys never told me about Instagram or selfies."

"Instagram?"

"Do you even use Instagram?"

"I'm not that active but of course."

"How many followers do you have?"

"Not really sure. Maybe 100?"

"A hundred followers?! Ugh. Roge would never let you into SSAFY."

"Roge?"

"Yes, Roge. Owner of SSAFY. He's so spiritual."

Ashwala looked a bit annoyed and said, "Eddie, that's not real yoga."

"I just took class there and it was by far the best class I've ever taken."

"You took class at SSAFY?!"

"And Roge is way more spiritual than Vishypu."

Ashwala grew more upset. "You sound ridiculous! Vishy is a true yoga master. Roge is a porn star!"

"No one here ever takes selfies."

"What are you talking about?"

"We took selfies, and I got spanked in Dog."

"Spanked?!"

"Yes! They said I'm super spiritual and they want me to take at least 100 selfies a day!"

"Who told you to take selfies in a yoga class?"

"Carly and Asia! Everyone at SSAFY takes selfies!"

"Eddie, you're ranting." Ashwala's eyes teared up. "Those two women aren't true yoginis. None of that is yoga. We should never allow them in here. They're ruining yoga. You need to connect with the breath and...."

"The breath, the Oms, the Namastes. None of that matters. I'm sorry, Ashwala. I just joined SSAFY! I want to quit this place so tell me what I have to do."

"YOU DID WHAT?!?!!"

"Um. I joined SSAFY. So yeah, I really want to end my contract, please."

"I don't believe it."

"Ashwala, you really should try it."

"You want me to try SSAFY?!"

"Roge told me to tell you to take his class."

"Roge is a pig. I will not step into that disgusting place. How could you!?"

"What?"

"You joined SSAFY?! Are you insane?!"

Ashwala's shift was over, and Tim, whose shift was starting, came in to take over. Feeling dejected and holding back tears, Ashwala walked away with her head down.

Tim smiled. "Checking in for class?"

"Actually, no. I joined SSAFY, and I would like to end my membership."

Tim's face turned bright red. "YOU JOINED SSAFY? THOSE IDIOTS WHO ALLOW NETFLIX AND SELFIES?!" he shouted.

Wow, Carly was right. This place is crazy.

"It was actually super spiritual. Way more spiritual than here."

Tim screamed. "GET THE FUCK OUT OF HERE NOW! GET OUT! GO! SECURITY!"

A loud siren blared overhead. Two yoga bouncers with handcuffs and mala beads made their way towards me.

"Mipu and Joshan. Escort Eddie out of here immediately. He is no longer welcome!"

Hearing the commotion, a group of yogis ran out from the yoga room. Tim was still bellowing.

"Eddie just joined SSAFY! QUICK, GET HIM!"

Yogis started throwing yoga bolsters at me. A foam block smacked me across the face just as Mipu and Joshan grabbed me by the arms.

A woman yelled out, "Tie him up in mala beads!"

Right before another block was about to strike, I broke free from Mipu and Joshan and sprinted out of there as fast as I could.

Tim was still screaming, "Get out, Eddie! Don't ever come back!"

"Yeah-yeah, whatever! Your Instagrams are awful! Have fun breathing and lying in stupid Savasana!"

When I got home, I checked my DMs and saw a new message from Carly. She had sent me two blue-heart emojis and two red-lip emojis, welcoming me to the SSAFY fam. 💙💜💋💋

I turned on the SSAFY Youtube channel, opened up my SSAFY brochures and spent the rest of the evening immersing myself in the world of SSAFY. I read about the different class styles, the upcoming workshops and the complex history of where SSAFY came from, and how Handstand and a yoga conference in Vegas helped bring SSAFY to life.

There was an SSAFY summer calendar featuring Jo, Misty, Carly, and Asia holding the most acrobatic yoga postures I had ever seen. Roge and Skone held erotic variations of Double Handstand and as I leafed through, I could feel my body start to tingle. Before I knew it, I threw on my new pink Speedo and worked on a few Speedo selfies. *Eddie, what the hell are you doing?! I want to try a Speedo selfie like Roge and Skone! Stop it! You're making the wrong choice! Go back to the Sanctuary and reinstate your membership. Apologize to Ashwala. No way! Post that Speedo selfie you hot sexy stud!*

With a touch of Brightness and the Lo-Fi filter, I posted my very first Speedo selfie. Right away, my phone buzzed. It was a DM from Asia:

> *"Eddie. I just saw your Speedo selfie! So spiritual! Pink looks hot on you. See you and your hot spiritual ass tomorrow."* 😋

CHAPTER 9
The sexy swami

"Go, Eddie, Go! Quick, everyone! Story Eddie! Stretch those legs higher in the air! Abs in! Strong core! Handstand, baby! You're doing it! Yes! Look at all the new followers! You just passed 100,000! Tag Eddie and tag SSAFY! You're spiritual as fuck, sexy yogis!"

The months went by, and I spent them living and breathing SSAFY (well, technically, I wasn't breathing since breathing wasn't allowed.) I made my way up to 100 selfies a day and reached 100,000 followers. I went to class #everydamnday, and within a few weeks, I managed to hold my first ever Dining Table Handstand at the Almond Nut. I still wasn't quite ready to take Handstand selfies, but Skone thought I was only a few weeks away. Asia taught me how to take selfies in each of the Standing Postures. I took Misty's bathtub meditation class every Friday night. They were much more spiritual than those silly sound baths at the Sanctuary. Jo's three-day workshop on belfies was super spiritual, and Gordo's ab classes every Monday, Wednesday, and Friday were the perfect way to start the morning. Carly was still my favorite teacher. All the teachers at SSAFY were spiritual AF, but I connected the most with Carly's tight leather yoga pants. Her spanks also felt way more spiritual than the other teachers at SSAFY.

I hadn't seen much of Ashwala or Vishypu lately. Sometimes I get a little bummed out thinking about all the time I wasted at the Sanctuary. So much emphasis on breathing and lying still when I should have been focused on IG and my abs. I still couldn't believe Vishypu never taught me how to hold Handstand or take an ab selfie. Then I thought of Ashwala and her pathetic 100 followers. How could anyone be the front desk manager at a yoga studio and not have at least 10,000 followers?

Asia, Carly, Skone, Gordo, Misty, and Jo were easily the most spiritual people I had ever met. We took Bird and sunset selfies together every Friday night, and they took me to all the exclusive SSAFY certified clubs, juice bars, and restaurants. Asia and Carly were the fan favorites for sure. They couldn't go anywhere without someone asking for an autograph, a spank, or a tip on how to be more spiritual. As for Roge, I hadn't seen him at the studio for a few days. Rumor had it he'd been away in Austin putting the finishing touches on a brand new SSAFY studio.

I was coming out of Skone's Dining Table Handstand workshop and about to go for a session of shower selfies. I grabbed a bottle of alkaline water and a cooling moist towelette at the bar when I overheard Misty and Johanna gossiping about something in the hallway.

I heard Misty say, "No way? In Austin? That's amazing!"

"It's going to be super spiritual. Roge told me it's super hot. Are you going to go for it?" asked Johanna.

"Gosh, I don't know. Roge hasn't asked. I kinda think he wants me focused on growing the Shower Yoga clientele. What about you, Jo? You'd be perfect. You're over a million followers, total six-pack. Everyone loves you."

"I don't think so. My belfie workshops are booked until the end of the year. My butt sponsors really want me pushing their new line of products."

"Sounds super hectic."

"And Melo started sponsoring me. They want a thong shot #everydamnday, and they want a Thailand and Maui thong shot every week. It's crazy!"

"Sounds like Gordo and Skone are next in line."

I kept walking down the hall when the critical voices came back. *Gordo and Skone? What about me? YOU?! HA! Come on. That's ridiculous. You really think Roge will ask you to be a Sexy Swami? You just learned Handstand. You barely got a six-pack last week. Gordo and Skone have like a million more followers than you. No way are you going to be the Sexy Swami in Austin.*

I jumped in the shower, turned on the video cameras, and opted for an IG Live and a few selfies of my bum. I figured I'd try out some of the tricks Jo taught me in her belfie workshop when Skone walked in. Instead of taking selfies, Skone sprung into One-Handed Handstand in the shower while using his other hand to rub soap over his chest.

"Skone. Today's workshop was awesome."

"Thanks, bro. You're killing it!"

"I can't wait to try Malibu Pier Handstand."

"Stoked! My sunset Handstand selfies go nuts on IG."

I noticed Skone wasn't taking any selfies. "Are you ok?" I asked and spat out some filtered shower water. "You're not taking selfies!"

"I'm working on some new Shower Handstands, bro. I'm trying to nail this new variation where I have soap all over my body and take this Soapy Shower One-Handed Handstand. Gordo is 50,000 followers ahead of me. I gotta catch up if I wanna get to Austin!"

"What's this with Austin everyone's talking about?"

"Dude. SSAFY is expanding," he said and proceeded to massage soap onto his now-not-so-private parts. "They're opening another studio, and they're looking for a new Sexy Swami. I have to get it."

Mental pictures of Austin flashed in front of my eyes. I saw Birds, electric bikes, and 6th St. The smell of Texas barbecue and the brand new SSAFY studio with me at the front of the room, wearing my hair in a man-bun like Roge. *Dude, snap out of it! What the heck is wrong with you? Get it out of your dumb head. You're not going to Austin! You're not even close to being a Swami! Look at Skone. Can you hold Shower Handstand? No. And look at his abs! You're not going anywhere, loser.*

"Sounds great, Skone! I'm sure you'll make a great Sexy Swami."

Skone didn't hear me. He came down from Handstand, took out his phone, and worked on some belfies. On my way out, I nearly tripped over Gordo. He was on the ground taking ab selfies and working on more sit-ups. "Gordo! Hey man, what's up?"

"Trying to keep the lead over Skone. I just reached 1.5 million followers. Gotta keep it going."

Gordo flipped over into Forearm Plank. "Bro, stand on my back while I hold this. Keep the Speedo on!"

"You sure?"

"Step on up. I'll tag you."

"Sweet. Thanks, man."

"Hey, have you seen Skone?"

"He's in the shower. Doing some belfies or some kind of Shower Handstand."

"Fuck, a new Shower Handstand? Did you see it? Was it spiritual?"

"It was pretty cool. He had all this soap on him. I don't know how he comes up with them."

"Was it two-handed or one-handed?"

"Pretty sure it was one-handed."

Still in Plank, Gordo opened up Instagram and found Skone's profile. There was a new post of Skone holding Shower Handstand with only one hand.

"That's hot. In the shower. Great lighting. Abs are tight. Nice filter, too. He's got some new tricks up his sleeves."

Gordo stood up, ripped off his shirt, flexed his abs, and took a few more ab selfies. "Yeah, but is he as hot as this?!"

"Whoa. Is that a ten-pack?"

"Fuckin-A it's a ten-pack. Skone doesn't have one of these, baby."

"You're totally going to be the next Sexy Swami."

"Almost there, bro. Once I get a twelve-pack, Austin is all mine."

I was lying on my couch, working on a few kitty cat selfies with Leo. I was reading about the SSAFY Limbs of Yoga when my mind went back to the new studio in Austin. I knew I didn't stand much of a chance at becoming the next Sexy Swami. It was a pretty ambitious goal for someone like me to be running a new SSAFY studio. I was only at 100,000 followers. I had just gotten a six-pack a couple of days ago, and there was Gordo with over a million followers, zeroing in on a twelve-pack. I barely knew how to hold Handstand, and there was Skone mastering some wild new variation of Shower Handstand. *You should ask Roge to consider you! Dude, no way! Gordo and Skone are way more spiritual than you! What is your hang-up on Austin? Forget it. You're not Swami material. You need to let it go.*

I hopped on Instagram and saw a new post from the official SSAFY account. It was a Live feed of Roge from the new SSAFY studio in Austin. He was sporting his iconic neon Speedos. Carly and Asia were wearing matching bikinis, doing Scorpion pose in the background while a sexy yogi assistant was rubbing massage oil over Roge's body. As usual, Roge's nut cleavage was bulging through his shorts as he looked to the camera.

"Sexy yogis! Exciting day for SSAFY as I officially get to announce the opening of a brand new SSAFY studio in Austin. SSAFY Austin will be the sexiest and most spiritual place in Texas. We're currently looking for some of Austin's hottest yoga teachers. If you have a six-pack and you can hold Handstand and you've completed at least ten hours of training, send me a DM with a few Handstand and ab shots. If you're SSAFY material, I'll hit you back. SSAFY Austin is going to be hot as fuck. Mirrors on every wall, kegs, a full bar, a rooftop sun deck and outdoor yoga. We're going to have five studio rooms, one dedicated to Bathtub and Shower Yoga, one room dedicated to abs, one dedicated to Handstands, one for the Heated Spank classes and one room dedicated to the Feather and Oil Flow. As for the new Sexy Swami in Austin, it's come down to two of my favorite teachers. Gordo and Skone, may the sexiest, most spiritual yogi win."

CHAPTER 10
A blowup doll, kettlebell and Gordo

Gordo grew up in a small Midwest town with a deep-rooted passion for acting from a young age. He starred as Huck Finn and Holden Caulfield in high school and had a short stint on Broadway playing one of the cats in *Cats*. He eventually made his way to LA to pursue his lifelong dream of acting, but after a few years, it became clear he was never going to "make it." One audition after another, Gordo was turned down, so he did what most failed actors do in Los Angeles. He took a two hundred-hour teacher training program and became a yoga teacher.

Gordo loved the physical demands of the practice, the student-teacher-dynamic, and how students lionized him, but more than anything, Gordo loved to teach because it allowed him to work on his craft as an actor. Gordo had been battling depression and anxiety for years, but he was fully committed to acting like a happy yogi the moment he walked into the yoga room. *Why was he so depressed?* A few years ago, Gordo was in Santa Monica Park, working on some new acro-yoga postures. When he went to lift his partner, Yellow, into the air with his feet, Gordo lost hold of her, and she landed awkwardly with her head hitting a kombucha bottle. Yellow wound up needing fifteen stitches and fractured both of her wrists. To this day, Yellow still can't hold a Handstand, and her practice hasn't been the same since.

This unfortunate accident weighed heavily on Gordo and only added to his excessive drinking and depression. Despite his keen ability to transform himself into a supportive, upbeat and enthusiastic yoga teacher, behind the hugs, the Handstands, and his impeccable abs, Gordo was still depressed AF.

When Gordo wasn't teaching yoga, he was at home on his couch drinking, staring at Instagram, and taking selfies. Night after night, selfies and Instagram. And the more he drank, Gordo spun even further down the rabbit hole of Instagram. He loved the filters and how they made his skin look silky smooth. He loved boomerangs, the stories, the emojis, and superzoom videos. He especially loved how IGTV made him feel like he was the star of his very own TV show. Instagram was everything to Gordo, and it was the perfect escape from his lonely and solitary life. That's why when Roge and the Vegas gang asked him to take ab selfies and use Instagram to promote SSAFY, Gordo was all in.

Gordo had always been in tip-top shape. He was a runner, a swimmer, and lifted weights six days a week, but more than anything, Gordo was obsessed with getting rock-hard abs. Gordo was convinced the world would be a happier and more spiritual place if everyone had a six-pack so he changed all of his SSAFY classes to ab classes. No flow, no standing postures, no stretching. Just abs.

For Instagram, Gordo created the inspirational ab selfie series with the hashtag #anabselfieadaykeepsthedoctoraway. The first week after joining SSAFY, he started out modestly, posting 50 ab selfies a day. The following week… 100. Then 200. Once word got out that the sexy yogi with the most followers would be the new Swami in Austin, Gordo was up to 300 ab selfies a day.

He was a true ab selfie artiste, creating various incarnations of the ab selfie unlike anything yogis had ever seen. Tanning salon ab selfies, shower ab selfies, kombucha ab selfies where he pours kombucha over his abs, and the infamous Salt & Straw ice cream ab selfie. Poké ab selfies where pieces of poké are gently placed on his abdominals. Soybean and matcha ab selfies.

One evening, Gordo was massaging and exfoliating his abs when he noticed a tingling sensation emanating from his groin. The more he massaged and stared at his abs, the sensations grew even stronger. To his surprise, Gordo was experiencing his very first ab selfie hard-on. In this wild moment of excitement, Gordo didn't know what to do next. Take a selfie? Pleasure himself? Both at the same time? Gordo opted to put his phone down (for once) and began to pleasure himself while staring at his abs. He caressed his belly with one hand and held his spiritual weiner with the other. He fantasized about followers eating poké off of his abs and rubbing soy sauce all over them. When he was finished, in a state of spiritual euphoria, Gordo went back to his phone, snapped another ab selfie, and added a dash of the Lo-Fi filter. When he went to post his ab pic, something took him by surprise. His ab selfie looked different.

The Instagram filter combined with the lighting and shadows from his abdominals created the illusion that Gordo was the proud owner of a twelve-pack! It didn't seem possible, but it was a gigantic milestone for Gordo and the entire SSAFY community. The very first twelve-pack ab selfie ever taken. Gordo posted his ab pic, and within seconds, his phone exploded with notifications. LIKE-LIKE-LIKE-LIKE. One after the other. Within seconds, his ab pic hit 50,000 likes. Another minute passed... 100,000 likes. It became the most spiritual ab selfie ever recorded on IG and the happiest day of Gordo's life. With just a few days left before Roge would officially announce the new Sexy Swami, Gordo was convinced with his twelve-pack, he'd be crowned as the winner.

To celebrate his momentous achievement, the next day Gordo scooted to the Venice Beach boardwalk to sign autographs and give fans a once-in-a-lifetime opportunity to take selfies while standing next to his abs. But even after a fun-filled day of posing with adoring fans, that night when Gordo stepped into his apartment, he could feel the depression and loneliness set back in. Gordo poured himself a shot of vanilla vodka, dimmed the lights, lit his favorite vanilla-scented candles, and returned to IG and more selfies. Hoping to recapture the joy he felt earlier at the beach, Gordo stared at his now infamous twelve-pack. He scrolled through the comments, looked at the tens of thousands of heart emojis, and once again he began to feel aroused.

With one hand stroking himself, Gordo reached for his phone and took another ab selfie right before he erupted all over his hand. Gordo quickly went back to IG, scrolled for his favorite Lo-Fi filter and added a touch of brightness to create what he thought would be that perfect twelve-pack selfie effect. But after a few moments of tweaking his favorite filter, and even with a little added saturation, there was still no sign of a twelve-pack. Frustrated AF, Gordo raised his phone above his abs and tried again. Selfie. More tweaking, more filtering but nothing. He tried again. And again. And again. Selfie, filter, adjustments.... Still no twelve-pack. *It's the lighting, Gordo! You need better lighting!* Gordo lit a few candles and held one directly above his abs, and tried another selfie. He looked again, but to his dismay, no sign of a twelve-pack.

12:15 AM. Gordo unrolled his workout mat, hit the floor and was off. Yoga bicycles. Left, right, left, right. Like a maniac, stretching his legs out, touching elbow to knee. Back and forth. A thousand yoga bicycles. He grabbed his phone and snapped another selfie. Still no twelve-pack! He took another shot of vanilla vodka and went back at it with more yoga bicycles.

12:45 AM. Leg lifts, swivels, and toe touches. He came down to his forearms and held a sixty-minute Forearm Plank. Gordo paused for another shot of vodka. He reached for his phone and took another ab selfie, and tried a few different filters. NOTHING! Like a lunatic, Gordo screamed, "FUCK! What's wrong with my abs?! Where did my twelve-pack go?!" *Go to bed, Gordo. Your abs are already sexy AF! NO! You need to keep the lead over Skone! Try rubbing some oil on your abs, Gordo! You need that oily silky effect!*

2:30 AM. Gordo took another shot of vanilla vodka and downed a Red Bull. He eyeballed his room and saw a bottle of baby oil on his dresser. He snatched it and squirted oil over his body. He then looked around and noticed his two fifty-pound kettlebells on the floor. *No, Gordo, don't do it! Your hands are too slippery! It's dangerous! You're drunk and tired. Go to sleep! What about the weighted blow-up doll? Yes, get the blow-up doll!* Gordo suddenly remembered his weighted, life-size blow-up doll in his closet.

Ever since the acro accident with Yellow, he uses it each night to practice acro yoga.

With a kettlebell in each hand and the blow-up doll under his arm, Gordo was ready to return to his mat and get back to work. Lying down, Gordo placed the thirty-pound blow-up doll between his legs and then grabbed his two kettlebells. He started with blow-up doll leg lifts. Up, down, up, down. *With the blow-up doll between his legs!? YES!* Simultaneously with the leg lifts, he started to do chest presses with the kettlebells. Up, down, up, down. With each leg lift and chest press, Gordo was determined to bring his twelve-pack back to life. His face red and grimacing, his abs burning, he was possessed and driven by just one thing… becoming the next Sexy Swami.

3:15 AM. While Gordo was immersed in his workout, all this time, Gordo's grey cat, Giovanni, had been peacefully lying in the far corner of the room, fixated on a small fly hovering overhead. Attracted to the scent of candles, sweat, and baby oil, the fly was circling around Gordo's body. Immersed in his workout, Gordo paid no attention to the pesky fly. On the other hand, staring intently, Giovanni was ready to pounce. In the midst of Gordo's chest press, the fly zoomed down and landed on his chest. At that very moment, Giovanni seized the opportunity, leaped across the room, and darted towards the fly. (Little did Giovanni know that Gordo's chest would be so slippery.) What happened next was a blur of fur, paws, kettlebells, and a blow-up doll. When Giovanni landed on Gordo's oil-slicked chest, his paws lost traction, and he slid and skidded into Gordo's face, missing the fly by a split second. Startled by the crash, Gordo lost his concentration while Giovanni scurried and hid under the bed. The kettlebells that Gordo had been gripping directly above his head slipped out of his hands and landed with a thud on his forehead.

Gordo's body instantly went limp. Blood dripped down the side of his face. The vanilla candles were still burning, adding to the eerie silence. Giovanni slowly crept out from under the bed, walked onto Gordo's belly, curled up into a little ball, and fell asleep.

10:00 AM. In a typical morning, Gordo averaged close to 200 ab selfies by 9:30. When Roge opened Instagram and didn't see a single ab selfie from Gordo, Roge immediately sensed something was wrong. Roge scooted over to Gordo's apartment as fast as he could. The front door was unlocked. When Roge walked in, Giovanni meowed and leaped into his arms. Roge could smell the scent of vanilla in the air as he walked towards the bedroom, calling out Gordo's name.

Opening the bedroom door, Roge screamed in horror. Gordo's body lay motionless in a pool of blood, a kettlebell on top of his head and the blow-up doll faced down, draped across his body. Roge raised his phone to take a quick cat selfie with Giovanni and then ran to see if Gordo was still alive. Roge shook Gordo's arms, trying to revive him, but it was too late. Gordo's arms were already ice-cold to the touch.

Roge lowered his ear to Gordo's chest to check for a heartbeat and realized Gordo was gone. Giovanni curled up on Gordo's belly, perhaps sensing this would be his last time snuggling up with his dad. Roge was about to call 911 but first lowered his head onto Gordo's chest next to Giovanni and took what would be the last selfie for Gordo's IG family. Roge brought Giovanni into his arms, lifted his phone and took another selfie-this time, a crying cat selfie.

CHAPTER 11

Blood, cats, and
Hard Kombucha

I was practicing some green juice selfies on the SSAFY sun deck when I heard the news. Misty, who had known Gordo since they first met in acting class, saw Roge's crying kitty cat selfie and could sense something was wrong. After posting his selfie, Roge went Live on IG from Gordo's apartment, sharing the news about how Gordo had presumably died trying to become the next Sexy Swami. Roge said he would anoint Giovanni the new SSAFY mascot, and promised to post a kitty cat ab selfie with Giovanni #everydamnday in memory of Gordo.

Misty was on the yoga mat next to me, trying out a new bikini selfie when she dropped her phone and let out a scream.

"What's wrong?!" I asked her.

"Look!" She shoved the phone in my face. "Look at Roge's cat selfie!"

"Oh, shit... is that... is that blood? Is Gordo dead? What happened?!"

"LOOK HOW MANY LIKES IT HAS! I AM TOTALLY BUYING A CAT!"

"What happened to Gordo?!"

"Wait, you have a cat!"

"Um, yeah, I have two."

"Please-please-please. Can I borrow them? I have to try cat selfies. Roge's cat selfie has over 100,000 likes!"

I was trying to listen to Roge on his IG Live, but Misty kept talking over him.

"Oh my God! I'll take selfies with both cats! Double cat bikini selfies! Have you taken a selfie with two cats at the same time?"

"Not really."

"I have to be first. Maybe I can come over later and practice? Do you ever take them for a drive? Like convertible cat selfies?"

"I don't know, Misty."

"Please-please-please?!"

"Fine… come take a bathtub selfie with them… whatever."

"Yes, a kitty cat bathtub selfie!"

Skyler came up to see what all the commotion was about. Misty showed her Roge's latest selfie from Gordo's bedroom.

"Wow, that's a lot of likes!"

"I know, right? I'm totally borrowing Eddie's cats. How could I not own a cat?!"

Skyler looked a bit shaken up by Roge's post. "Wow, I'm going to miss Gordo's abs. They were so spiritual."

Misty agreed. "Totally. I wonder who's going to teach his ab classes? No one comes close to abs like Gordo's."

Just then, Carly and Skone walked onto the sundeck and joined us.

"Carly! Skone!" I called out. "Have you heard?"

"Yeah, I can't believe it…." Carly took a sundeck selfie then removed her sunglasses as she shook her head in disbelief.

"Roge set a new record with likes. Guarantee we have a cat selfie workshop next week."

Misty yelled, "I'm borrowing Eddie's cats tonight!"

Carly squawked, "No fair! I want dibs."

I still couldn't believe no one was talking about Gordo. "Does anyone know what happened to Gordo!?"

Skone hopped into a Kombucha Handstand and yelped, "Looks like I'm the new Sexy Swami, baby!"

Carly looked up to Skone. "Not so fast, Skone. Still have to get over 2 million followers. Last I checked, you were still around 1.6."

"Don't worry, Carly. Eddie and I are going to the Malibu Pier for some Sunset Pier Handstands. I'll hit 2 million easy."

Carly looked at me and smiled, "Wow, Eddie. Doing the old Pier Handstands, eh?"

"I figured I'd give it a try."

"Hey, Skone. You better look out! Sexy Eddie may be giving you a run for the Swami position in Austin."

Skone came down from his keg stand and joined the rest of the group. "Well, it's a shame about Gordo. But at least Roge came up with a new selfie, and Gordo died an SSAFY hero."

Misty was still curious about the new selfie trend. "You think Roge is working out the metrics yet? Like where the cat should be in comparison to the abs. What filter looks best with the cat? Does it matter what color the cat is?"

With frazzled energy, Misty grabbed my arm. "What color are your cats?!"

"Leo is grey, and Nellie is orange."

Carly tried to reassure the group that everything would be okay. "Guys, I promise, when Roge comes back to the studio, he'll have it all figured out. You know he wants cat selfies to be spiritual and sexy as fuck."

Misty couldn't stop looking at Roge's new creation. "He really is incredible. Why didn't I think of that pose!? It's up to 200,000 likes!"

"They don't call him the guru for nothing!" Skone chuckled as the rest of us burst into laughter. Carly walked to the bar and ordered a round of wheatgrass shots. Everyone raised their phones and shots high and proceeded with more selfies, spurred on by Roge's new like record.

"To Gordo's abs."

"To Gordo's abs and Giovanni!"

"I guess that means we got ourselves a new Sexy Swami in Austin," Carly said casually as all eyes were at once on Skone.

I left the studio without taking any shower selfies that day. I had a funny feeling in my stomach. Roge had broken some kind of cat selfie record, but I couldn't help but wonder why I hadn't taken more cat selfies? Misty was right. How could I be so stupid? All this time with two cats and I'm stuck on one cat selfie a day. I should have been happy for Roge and Giovanni. This new cat selfie trend may be just what I need. With Leo and Nellie, there's no reason why my IG shouldn't explode. I even wondered if Roge will ask me to teach a new cat selfie workshop, but then I couldn't stop thinking about the image of Gordo's battered head and the blood dripping from his forehead. Could Roge have saved Gordo?

Does Roge even like cats? Why hadn't Roge told me to take more cat selfies? Doesn't he know I own two cats?

Misty was walking out of the lobby when she saw me standing by the door with my head down.

"All this sulking is killing my vibe," she sighed. "Look, I'm sure Roge will find someone whose abs look just as sexy as Gordo's."

"It's really a drag."

"The ab classes aren't going anywhere."

"No, I feel bad for Gordo."

"We're all gonna miss Gordo's abs but no sense to be a Debbie Downer about it!"

"Does anyone know what happened?"

"You know what you need!? A gin-infused kombucha. I know just the place..."

Misty took me to a new SSAFY-certified hard kombucha bar a few blocks away. The rest of the SSAFY crew were already there, talking about new incarnations of the now infamous cat selfie. Skyler was facetiming with an SSAFY-certified cat shelter asking about the different colored cats. Skone was talking about trying a new variation of Handstand while holding a cat. Carly suggested a Friday night yoga dance party at the local cat shelter. Roge could tell I wasn't myself and egged me on to have another drink.

"Eddie, you're golden, bro. You have two cats. If you play this right, you're going to be a freaking star."

"I guess you're right, Roge."

"You could do Warrior Two with a cat in both hands. Warrior One with cats above your head. A hot Cat Flow or maybe Down Dog or Plank Pose with cats on your back."

Misty yelled out, "Call it Down Cat!"

Carly shouted, "Make Eddie the Cat Yoga Guru!"

Everyone cheered and jumped into Handstand while Misty went back to kombucha selfies. When it turned into one big Handstand party, I got up from the table and stumbled towards the exit. I took one more sip of kombucha and found myself at the back of the bar. I had to walk around and go through an alleyway to get to the main street. There were glass bottles and soggy cardboard boxes on the ground. I stumbled and fell over and bumped my head on a trash bin. Buzzed, hurt, and a bit disoriented, I sat on the ground, not quite sure what hit me. *Eddie, look at you. You're a mess. What is the matter with you? You should be in there with the gang holding Handstand.* Fuck, there was that critical voice again. But this time, it sounded different. It wasn't "my" voice!

"Who's there!?" I called out.

You should be practicing your Handstands and working on your abs. And don't let Misty near your cats! You're the real innovator of cat selfies. Take a double cat ab selfie with Nellie and Leo. You could be the Sexy Swami. I have great faith in you.

Gordo? Is that you?

Eddie, yes, it's me. Your Ab Guru. You're drunk, and you've bumped your head. You've had a long day and a few too many hard kombuchas. Go home. Get some sleep. Hug your kitties. I see great things from you. You can do it.

What was Gordo talking about? Do what? Was he still alive?

In the morning, take at least 200 selfies with your cats. Your cats are way more spiritual than Giovanni. Take pillow cat selfies. Smoothie and coffee cat selfies. Wash your face cat selfies. Nipple cat selfies and let them lick your nipples. Hundreds of selfies. As many as you can. Then work on those abs. A thousand yoga bicycles. Take my ab class on YouTube. Abs and cats. You can do it. You're sexy as fuck. This is your chance.

But what about Skone? He's way more spiritual than I am.

Eddie. You're just as spiritual. I have faith in you.

When I finally arrived home, I opened up IG and stumbled to bed. Nellie and Leo hopped up and joined me as I thought about what Gordo had said. Maybe he was right. Maybe I was the Sexy Swami SSAFY Austin needed. Why should I let Misty take selfies with both of my cats? Why should Roge get all the credit for the first cat ab selfie? I had been taking cat selfies for months. Nellie and Leo both closed their eyes and plopped their heads down on a pillow. I raised my phone and took a kitty cat nighttime pillow selfie, and waved good-bye to Instagram. I closed my eyes and fell asleep as soon as my head hit the pillow.

I woke up with a terrible headache. I grabbed my phone and looked at my cat selfie: 590,000 likes. I looked at Roge's selfie with Giovanni: 472,000 likes. Gordo was right. My cat selfie was way more spiritual than Roge's, AND I was over 240,000 followers. Nellie and Leo still had their eyes closed. I tried to wake them up and share my excitement, but they were fast asleep. I thought I had dreamt everything, but then Gordo's voice came back. *Go to SSAFY and tell them you can be the next Sexy Swami! Take all the Handstand workshops you can and go take Sunset Pier Handstand with Skone. Wear the camouflage Speedos. Don't forget to tag me. I'm dead, but I'm still using Instagram.*

I sprung out of bed and downed a few shots of wheatgrass and a carrot juice. I put on my red and white camouflage Speedos and put my face right between Leo and Nellie while they slept. After a couple hundred cat selfies, I hit the floor and worked on my abs, hoping Nellie and Leo would join me. Gordo's voice came back.

Eddie. Your cats are still asleep. Go out and take some scooter and beach selfies. Maybe some sunrise juice selfies.

I took Gordo's advice, threw on a new SSAFY thong, and darted out for a run. I stopped every couple of minutes for more selfies; butt, crotch, and duck lip selfies. Juice and granola selfies. Smoothie and sand selfies. Cappuccino and scone selfies. Nothing could stop me as my growing confidence was given a new boost. The likes and heart emojis were raining in. I paused the selfies for a moment to call the SSAFY studio.

"Yeah, it's Eddie. Sign me up for every SSAFY class there is. And every ab and Handstand workshop on the schedule, put me in. Front row!"

CHAPTER 12
DON'T TRY THIS AT HOME

"**Y**ou guys! Look! Sexy Eddie is holding Handstand on top of a scooter! He looks sexy as fuck!"

The rest of the studio stopped in their tracks and ran up to the window where Skyler was standing with her nose pressed against the glass. Carly and Asia came down from Scorpion and glanced out to the street where, lo and behold, there I was, Handstanding on top of a Bird scooter.

"He looks so spiritual," chimed Asia.

"Look at his abs," cheered Johanna.

"So proud of him. He's my favorite student," added Carly.

Only Skone crossed his arms over his chest and puffed, "Oh, come on. Scooter Handstand is old news. I've been doing that for a year. I came up with that pose. Can he drink a smoothie at the same time?"

Asia could sense Skone was feeling jealous. "Look at Skone, getting nervous. Maybe Eddie can be the Austin Sexy Swami."

Carly added, "Good idea, Asia. Maybe a little Scooter Handstand contest on the pier."

Skone was growing more upset. "No-no. I have way more followers than him. I'm at 1.5 million followers! No, wait; 1.6. I'll be at 2 by the end of the weekend. I'm the Sexy Swami. And his abs are disgusting."

Carly continued, "Looks like he has a sexy six-pack to me."

Growing more agitated, Skone yelled, "Twelve-pack, Carly. Roge said you need a twelve-pack. Gordo and I are the only twelve-pack sexy yogis ever. Six-packs are for amateurs. I'm the Swami!"

Asia looked outside and said, "Guys, look! Eddie's doing Handstand on top of Carly's convertible!"

Oohs and ahhs echoed from the lobby as all eyes were on me.

Carly grabbed her keys and ran to the door. "Skyler! Come on. Gotta post this Live. I'll drive him up and down Main St. He'll hit 500,000 followers for sure."

Asia shouted, "We should do a Convertible Handstand workshop next week! This'll be great promo! GO EDDIE! Great work, sexy yogis!"

As Skyler and Carly ran outside, Skone was beginning to lose his temper. "I came up with Shower Handstand. I started Handstand on a bike. On a sea turtle. I was the first to do Handstand at the Fox Tower. At the mall! I did Handstand with my legs dangling out the window at the Wynn! I have fifty sponsors! Eddie has ZERO! Why is everyone going nuts over a freaking Scooter Handstand?! I own Scooter Handstand!"

Misty had heard enough. "Just zip it, Skone. We get it. You're fucking spiritual. You and your dumb Handstands."

"You're just jealous!"

"Am not!"

"Oh, please. You're the only one here who can't hold a freaking Handstand."

"So what!"

"It's pathetic. How can you call yourself a sexy yogi?"

"Big whoop, you can do a Handstand."

Skone wouldn't let up. "Roge should have never let you teach here. Shower Yoga?! Ha. I can do Shower Yoga with my eyes closed."

Misty was fuming. "You were the one who suggested Shower Yoga!"

"No, I said Bikini Yoga! Big difference."

"You said Shower Yoga!"

"Anyone can do yoga in a stupid shower! But I'm the only one who can do Shower Handstands!"

"Stop it! No one cares about Handstands!"

"I do. And so do my 1.6 million followers."

Roge strutted into the studio wearing no shirt and a new zebra-patterned thong. Despite being engrossed in crotch selfies, he could sense the awkwardness between Skone and Misty.

"Guys, you should be celebrating. Did you see Eddie? He's nailing Convertible Handstand. The guy's a stud."

Misty was still pouting, "Skone doesn't think I'm spiritual cause I can't hold Handstand!"

Skone piped in, "I'm just saying I should get a little more credit for coming up with Scooter Handstand. And convertible. Eddie's doing my pose!"

Roge tried to ease the tension. "Skone, what did we talk about? Misty's love jugs make her just as spiritual as you."

Glaring at Skone, Misty said, "See, told you."

Skone replied, "I just think it's a little unfair that she can claim to be just as spiritual as me and still not know how to hold a Handstand. I mean come on, Roge. At some point she's gotta learn the dang pose."

"Skone, I love your Handstands, brother. But can you do Bikini Yoga like Misty?"

"Well, no."

Misty couldn't hold back. "SEE! I'm just as spiritual as you! I could be the next Swami for all you know!"

Roge continued with his spiritual pep talk and added, "We can all be sexy and spiritual as fuck. Handstand. Breasts. Crotch and camel toe selfies. Belfies. The Threesome Flow. It's ALL spiritual. You're losing focus, Skone."

Roge leaned in and gave Skone and Misty an SSAFY squeeze. "Come on, no fighting at SSAFY. You should be storying Eddie. Gotta help him get 500,000 followers. He's one of our best students. Tag him."

Misty took out her phone, but Skone still looked peeved.

Roge looked to Skone and said, "Skone, what's going on?"

"It's just... Carly was saying that maybe Eddie would be the next Sexy Swami, and I don't think that's fair. I mean, you said it was me or Gordo, and now that Gordo's gone, I should be the Sexy Swami. I have way more followers. I have the abs. I can hold Handstand for days. I'm the Swami. LOOK AT ME. I'm a Swami."

Roge put his hand on Skone's shoulder." Of course you are, bud."

"Everyone keeps saying Eddie could be the Swami."

"Skone, relax. Just get to 2 million, and the Swami job is yours."

"I'm trying, Roge. I think I've hit a wall."

"What do you mean?"

"Like, I've done all the Handstands I can think of. I'm out."

"Venice Canal Bridge?"

"Yes, of course."

"On top of my speed boat?"

"Yes."

"Bus Handstand.'

"Yes."

"PCH Handstand?"

"Yep."

"Hollywood sign?"

"Yes. I'm telling you, man. I'm out of Handstands."

Roge paused for a moment. He was about to offer another suggestion but hesitated.

"What is it, Roge? Tell me!"

"It's too dangerous."

"Tell me!"

"Ok! Spire Handstand!"

"Wait, where?"

"The pier. The clock tower with the spire on top. Dude, that would be spiritual as fuck! Our Instagram would go nuts! You'd hit 2 million FOR SURE!"

Wrapped in Carly's arms, I made my way back inside the SSAFY studio surrounded by a crowd of sexy yogis. Asia and Skyler kept tagging me in selfies. Everyone was screaming my name. "EDDIE! EDDIE! EDDIE!"

Carly and I glided towards Roge and Skone when Carly said, "Roge, are you sure you don't want to throw Eddie in the Swami mix? He is looking spiritual as fuck!"

Skone's face was turning red. "ROGE! SEE!"

Carly and Asia were snickering.

Asia joined in on the fun and said, "Yeah, Roge. How about a little Handstand contest on the pier! Whoever's Handstand gets the most likes is crowned the new Swami!"

Skone cried out, "I'm the Sexy Swami! It's me! Eddie is not a Swami!"

Skone ripped off his shirt, "Look at these abs! Twelve-pack!"

He then hopped into One-Handed Handstand and blurted out, "Can Eddie do this?! NO!"

Skyler went, "I vote for Eddie!"

"And me!"

"Eddie!"

"I vote for Eddie!"

Skone came down from Handstand, grabbed me by the Speedo, and pulled me up close. 'That's it. YOU, ME, THE CLOCK TOWER! NOOOOWWWWWWWW!!!!!"

There was a golden-colored haze covering the sky as the sun set over the Pacific. Skone had already made his way up to the top of the clock tower. There was a rave-like atmosphere on the pier. Strobe lights, body paint, and glow sticks. Hundreds of shirtless sexy yogis dressed in thongs, Speedos, and bikinis dancing, twerking, taking Sunset Handstands, and group selfies. Asia and Carly, dressed in all leather, were holding double Handstand on the merry-go-round. Skyler was teaching her patented Oil Flow to the crowd. "Thong Song" pumped into the sky while Roge stood there in a leopard-skinned thong proudly overseeing the sea of yogis. With a cleanly shaven chest, he had a huge grin on his face as yogis leaned in next to his meat bags for more booty short selfies. Just a few months ago, Roge was saying goodbye to a banging career in porn, and now he was preparing to crown a new Sexy Swami. SSAFY was officially the most successful style of yoga ever created, and Roge was the mastermind. Last he checked, SSAFY surpassed 3 million followers and had earned 285 new sponsors.

As I looked up and saw Skone about to flip upside down into Spire Handstand, I felt the wheatgrass and carrot juice gurgling in my stomach. My heart started to pound out of my chest. The critical voices came back at a level I had never experienced before.

What the fuck are you doing?! Are you insane?! You're going to kill yourself! Get out of here! NOW!

Then Gordo's voice took over and shouted positive mantras.

You're the Sexy Swami, Eddie. You can do this. Your abs are sleek and sexy. You are the Sexy Swami.

Holding Giovanni, Roge came up from behind me and took a few more cat selfies.

"Awe, man. Eddie. Fucking huge day for SSAFY! So proud of you. Where are your cats?"

"My cats?"

"Dude, triple cat ab selfies!"

"Seriously, Roge?"

"Fuck yeah. I figured you'd have them with you when you did Handstand."

"My cats are at home, Roge."

"Well, next time. Come on, let's get a good view. You ready to get up there?! SSAFY BABY!"

Roge walked off into the crowd and started to dance. I gazed up at the Clock Tower and caught sight of something neon green. I looked closer, and there he was!

Skone, dressed in a bright green fluorescent Speedo, was holding Handstand on top of the Clock Tower! Hanging upside down, Skone grabbed a megaphone and screamed to the crowd, "UP HERE! TAG ME! I'M THE SEXY SWAMI!!!!"

Roge jumped on the DJ stage, grabbed the microphone, and yelled out to the electric crowd, "TAG SSAFY!! TAG SKONE! YOU ARE ALL SEXY AND SPIRITUAL AS FUCK! SKONE! SKONE! SKONE!"

The bass thumped as the music grew even louder. Strobe lights shone right into my eyes. Sexy yogis were bumping and grinding from every direction when the voices in my head came back again.

EDDIE, GET OUT OF THERE! SSAFY ISN'T WORTH IT! LOOK AT YOU. WHAT ARE YOU DOING?

I looked up and saw Skone reach for his phone. He managed to get it out without much trouble, but as he was fiddling with getting the password in, he wobbled. The rest of the crowd wasn't paying any attention.

"Skone, be careful!" I shouted.

But it was too late.

"I'm the Sexy Swamiiiiiiiiiiiiiiii…" Attempting the first-ever Spire Handstand selfie, Skone lost his balance and dropped his phone. He then flew off the tower, hitting the pier with a sickening thud.

"Skooooooone!"

I ran as fast as I could, but there were too many yogis blocking my way. I found Asia and Carly and tried to tell them what had happened but they were busy dancing and signing autographs. I ran towards the stage and found Roge, but he was immersed in another Thong Flow.

I yelled out, "ROGE! WE HAVE TO CALL THE AMBULANCE! SKONE FELL!"

Roge bent down to try and hear me.

"What's that Big-E?!"

"I SAID, SKONE FELL OFF THE TOWER!"

Roge was quiet for a moment. He looked up to the tower and then looked back at me. He reached into his pocket and took out his phone. Roge had a worried look on his face as he swiped left, right, up, and down. Finally, he leaned in and asked, "Did Skone not post his Handstand on Instagram?!"

"I can't hear you!"

"Do you know if Skone managed to post a selfie before he fell?"

"WHAT?!"

Roge yelled, "DID SKONE TAKE A FREAKING SELFIE? WHEN HE FELL?!"

"I'm not sure!"

"DID HE AT LEAST GO LIVE? TELL ME SOMEONE GOT THIS ON VIDEO! DID ANYONE TAG SKONE?!"

"I... no... I don't know, Roge!"

The voices came back again but louder and more cryptic.

You're next, loser. Don't think you're getting out of this alive. And when you die, no one will care because they'll all be taking selfies of their crotch. Your choice, Eddie. Get out of here or die like Gordo and Skone.

I was shaking and crying uncontrollably. A light rain began to fall as I took off away from the pier. I ran down Main Street as fast as I could to get away from what I had just seen and made it to my old stomping grounds, the Yoga Sanctuary of Spiritual Bliss. If I was lucky, I still had time to catch Ashwala before she finished her last shift.

The studio door was shut. There were wooden boards covering the windows. I knocked on the door.

"Ashwala!" I shouted.

Then I heard a voice behind me.

"She's not here."

I turned around. It was Vishypu.

"Vishypu!" I cried out. "I need a normal yoga class, I have to see Ashwala and tell her I'm sorry! I miss your classes! I miss the Sanctuary!"

"Ashwala left. The studio is permanently closed."

"I don't understand."

"No interest. Phones. Selfies. Students want to watch Netflix. They'd ask me to teach them how to take selfies and get more followers. I don't teach selfies. I don't even own a cell phone."

"Seriously?"

"No one cares about the breath. They'd leave before Savasana. It's over. Yoga is no more, Eddie."

I stood in the rain with my mouth wide open.

"What are you going to do?"

"Maybe a sabbatical or a Vipassana."

"And what about Ashwala? She wanted to go on your retreat."

"With the studio closed, the retreat's on hold. I haven't seen Ashwala for a few weeks. Last I heard, she had to give up her apartment."

Vishypu glanced down and noticed my Speedos.

"You look good, Eddie. Strong."

"Namaste, Vishypu."

"Remember to breathe, Eddie. Life isn't about how you look. It's about how you breathe. Your presence in the moment. Like right now. This moment. Nice to see you…"

Vishypu bowed his head and then walked off into the pouring rain.

It was getting late. I wandered the streets alone. I thought of
my first class at the Sanctuary, meeting Ashwala and her hand
massage. The sound baths, Vishypu's mala beads and how much
I missed the smell of incense. I stopped at an organic tea cafe. I
was still crying as I took a sip of my green tea, when suddenly,
my phone rang. It was Ashwala.

"Hello?"

"Eddie, I'm at Cafe Thankful. Can you come?"

CHAPTER 13
showdown

When I entered the cafe, Ashwala was sitting at a table in the corner. Roge was with her. They were talking about something over a Mint Cacao Chip Smoothie.

"Ashwala!" She looked up at me and smiled. I glanced at Roge. "Hey, Roge. Sorry about Skone."

With his face flinching, Roge replied, "I don't want to talk about it."

There was an awkward silence, then Roge continued. "I mean how the fuck does he not think to take a freaking selfie!?"

"Who, Skone?"

"YES! He does like 200 Handstands a day. Every time I see him, he's doing a damn Handstand! He takes like 300 selfies a day, and you mean to tell me he forgets to take a fucking Handstand selfie?!"

"He probably didn't want to fall."

"He ruined Spire Handstand! He set SSAFY back at least 100,000 followers!"

"Did you check his phone? Maybe he took one?"

"It's in the ocean! I come up with a once-in-a-lifetime posture, and he doesn't think to post a selfie before he falls! And... and... and... NO ONE tagged him!" Roge was incensed. "Hundreds of sexy yogis on the pier dancing, and no one tags him?!"

"So that's it?"

"Yes, because no one tagged him or took any videos! Skone and his Handstand. Both gone. I'm sending a DM to SSAFY members tonight. Emergency DM. When someone is holding a Handstand on a bridge, a skyscraper, on a car, or on top of a clock tower, you shoot a damn video!"

Roge was scrolling through his phone and still upset. "It's okay. I'm hiring a full-time camera crew for all SSAFY events. We'll just make sure this never happens again. Not going to let Skone ruin my vibes." Roge looked up from his phone and stared right at me. "I'm sorry you didn't get your chance to hold Spire Handstand."

"It's okay."

"No, it's not, Big-E. You've been a great student and Skone ruined it for SSAFY and for you. I want to make it up to you!"

Ashwala was fidgeting and noticeably uncomfortable. Roge gathered himself and exclaimed:

"The Big Sexy-E! Ash. You two are going to love this. Eddie, sit down. I've got some BIG news!"

I took a seat and grabbed a few pine nuts that were in a bowl on the table.

"You'll never guess whom I've asked to go to Austin?"

I raised an eyebrow.

"Ash! Our girl! The one and only! You're looking at the new front desk manager at SSAFY Austin!" He put his arm around Ashwala.

"Wow."

"Yeah, awesome, right!?" Roge beamed.

"Seriously?"

"Serious as a heart attack, Big-E."

Ashwala still hadn't said a word.

"I thought about it, and she's perfect! She's experienced, smart. Her hand massages are incredible! The moment you walk into the studio, BAM! Hand massage! I've been teaching her some hand selfie tricks. She's up to 12,000 followers! Trying out some new massage hashtags. She's a natural beauty which, as you know, is a big part of SSAFY."

Ashwala had been staring down at her drink while Roge was talking.

"Which means, Eddie, it's time to discuss the Sexy Swami opening. With Gordo and Skone both out…"

"They're dead, Roge."

"Skone, yes. Gordo…at least I got a selfie with him so he's technically not dead. As I was saying, with Gordo and Skone in a better place, the job is yours, brother."

"You're serious?"

"You're the Sexy Swami! You and Ash. Together in Austin."

"I don't know, Roge."

"You two are going to kill it. Dude, I saw that Handstand you took on Carly's car. That was spiritual as fuck, man. Your abs looked super spiritual. Lift up your shirt. Show Ash your abs!"

"I thought I needed a twelve-pack?"

Roge took out his phone and took a few quick shots of my abs and threw them on IG.

"Your six-pack slays. SSAFY loves you! These shots are getting tons of likes."

"So I'm the Swami?"

"Dude, you're a Swami natural." Roge looked at Ashwala and said, "Ash, isn't Eddie spiritual as fuck?"

Ashwala forced a smile and took a sip of her smoothie. Just then, Asia, Misty, and Carly walked in. Roge got up and met them at the bar.

I took Roge's seat next to Ashwala.

"You're going to Austin!? To work at SSAFY?!"

Ashwala shrugged and said, "I thought you'd be happy."

"This is insane! And I thought you hated Roge."

"Roge wants to help me."

"Ashwala, these people are crazy. Yogis are dying at SSAFY."

"I don't care. Vishypu closed the Sanctuary. I lost my job. What else was I going to do?"

"I don't think you understand what kind of people you're getting involved with."

"Look who's talking?! I think I remember telling you the same thing and YOU told me to stick it and that my Instagram sucked."

"Ash, this is a bad idea."

"Look, I know I've said unflattering things about SSAFY, but Roge offered me a job and he's helping my Instagram."

"But you hate Instagram!"

"I know! But I told him no thong selfies and he's cool with it. He's focusing me on eye and massage selfies." Ashwala sighed. "It's only temporary."

"You sure you can deal with Roge?"

"I'll be fine and I can save up money and go on the retreat with Vishypu in the fall. Just don't tell him I'm doing SSAFY. Vishy would kill me."

"I'm just nervous something's gonna happen to you!"

Ashwala's eyes softened.

"Then..." she said, "Come with me to Austin. You heard Roge. Be the Swami!"

Roge, Carly, Misty, and Asia came back to the table.

"Sooo..." Carly went. "Austin, huh?" she glared at Ashwala, who replied with a polite smile.

"That's funny, I thought SSAFY wasn't quote real yoga," snorted Asia.

Roge could sense the cattiness. "Asia, Carly. Ash here is going to be front desk manager in Austin with a focus on hand massages and eye selfies. You have to let her massage your hands. She's amazing!"

Growing more perturbed, Carly asked, "How many followers does she have?"

Roge replied, "I'm working on that."

Carly asked again, "Roge, how many followers does she have?"

Misty jumped in, "Yeah, Roge. How many followers?"

"I got her up to like 15,000 in ten minutes."

"Yuck." Carly had a dirty look on her face. "What about Handstands?"

"For sure. She'll do plenty of those, too."

With a devilish smirk, Asia sat down next to Ashwala. "Yeah, well let's see it."

Ashwala quickly tried to change the subject. "Roge was just telling me about the SSAFY studio. He showed me your Instagram and your Handstands, and the outfits you wear. I don't know how you do that. I'm really impressed."

Carly let her guard down a bit and smiled. "Well, that's sweet. We've put a lot of thought into filters and selfie angles. Lighting and whether to use gifs or emojis. Instagram has so many tools to learn. It's exhausting..."

Asia added, "…and the clothes. Ugh, so much thought on clothes, and do we do boomerangs or videos or just a selfie. We can show you if you want."

Ash smiled and said, "Yeah, I'd like that."

Roge raised his smoothie glass in the air.

"I propose a toast! To Ash and Eddie and the new SSAFY studio manager and the new Sexy Swami!"

Asia cheered, "To Handstands!"

Carly yelled, "TO SSAFY!"

Misty's face turned bright red. She was the only one who didn't lift her glass.

"ROGE! What did you say?!"

"Come on, Misty. Raise the smoothie glass. Let's toast."

Still enraged, Misty exclaimed, "Who is the Sexy Swami, Roge?!"

"Misty, relax."

"Don't tell me to relax! Who is the Swami?! What did you do?!"

"I thought I told you."

"No…no…You never told me."

"Big-E. Sexy Swami Eddie."

"WHAT?!"

"He's going to be dope!"

"You're the dope! I thought I'd be the Swami!"

Roge answered, "Sorry, but you can't hold Handstand and that's a no-no if you want to be a Swami."

Misty was growing more infuriated. "You said Shower Yoga was just as spiritual as a Handstand! I heard you, you said it!"

"We're all sexy and spiritual as fuck, but a Swami has to know how to hold Handstand."

Carly and Asia put their arms around Misty to try and console her.

"It's okay. We need you here in LA."

Misty yelled, "It's not okay! I have more followers than Eddie. Austin is going to have a Shower Yoga studio. You told me I could have my own Shower Yoga Studio."

Roge grabbed Misty's hand and said, "And you will, babe."

Misty screamed, "I have a six-pack!!!!"

Roge answered, "So does Eddie."

Misty stepped in closer and glared directly at me. "Alright, mother fucker. How many followers do you have?!"

"Uh… uh…"

"I said, Little Man. How many followers do you have?"

"Like 1.5 million."

"*Roge!* I have 1.7 million followers! This is not fair! I should be the Swami!"

Suddenly, Roge raised both of his arms and closed his eyes. "Wait, hold it!"

Asia and Carly looked at each other confused.

"What's wrong, Roge?"

"You okay?"

Misty whined, "Come on, Roge. Am I the Swami or what?"

With his eyes still closed and his hands in the air, Roge said, "In an SSAFY flow state. I'm feeling spiritually inspired… Hold on…"

Carly and Asia looked at him like a dog waiting for a treat from its master. Ashwala and I looked at each other, unsure what to think. Losing her patience, Misty looked like she was about to rip Roge's head off.

Roge finally opened his eyes. He took off his tank-top and pulled down his trousers to reveal a polka-dot thong and screamed, "SSAFY CONTEST TIME! EDDIE VS. MISTY! SSAFY SHOWDOWN! Whoever gets to 2 million followers first will be crowned the new Sexy Swami!"

Carly and Asia cheered. "GO-GO-GO!"

"YAY!"

I turned to Roge, "A contest?"

Misty grabbed me by the Speedos, "Oh you wussing out Little-E?" Misty turned to Roge. "See! What kind of Swami would wuss out on a contest?! Roge, you saw it! Eddie's wussing out!"

"I'm not wussing out. This is ridiculous."

Roge replied, "It's the only way, brother."

Misty took off her leather jacket and LOLO sweatpants. She wore a see-through black and mesh top and a bikini bottom. She grabbed a pitcher and poured water over her hair and skin. She then took out her phone and started taking selfies.

Ashwala jumped from her seat and yelled, "No fair. Misty already started!"

With a smirk, Misty said, "Oops. Looks like I'm at 1.8 million followers!"

Carly and Asia looked at me. "Go, Eddie! You gotta go!"

Misty was immersed in some of the sexiest and most spiritual chest and fanny selfies ever taken at Cafe Thankful. People quickly gathered and cheered Misty on.

Misty screamed out, "Follow me! Tag Mistyshoweryoga! Austin, here I come!"

Ashwala darted towards me with a look of distress. "What are you doing? You have to start taking selfies! She's going to win! I don't want to work in Austin with Misty!"

"I can't keep up with that!"

"Take some ab selfies. Take a Handstand! You have to win!"

Carly and Asia were flanking Misty and holding Handstand. With a possessed look, Misty was still screaming out her IG handle while taking selfie after selfie. Roge had a big smirk on his face when he saw me with my arms down by my side.

"You better get going, brother. Misty's got you beat!"

Ashwala begged, "Can't you help him, Roge?"

"I'm afraid it's all up to Big-E."

The critical voices came back. *Once a loser. Always a loser. Lame Eddie strikes again. Standing there like a wuss! No way are you a Swami! Eddie, snap out of it! Ashwala wants you in Austin! You are blowing it! Take some selfies, NOW!*

The same old critical voices continued when all of a sudden, I heard the voice of someone new. It was Skone. He spoke to me in a whisper.

Eddie. Handstand on the Bar.

There was too much cheering and screaming. I couldn't hear him. Talk louder, Skone. I can't hear you.

Handstand on the bar.

What did you say?

This time he yelled. *Eddie, wake up! Do Handstand on the Bar! Mint Cacao Chip Handstand on the Bar! It's the most popular smoothie. You can do it!*

Then I heard Gordo's voice.

Listen to Skone. He's right. The Mint Cacao Chip is everyone's favorite. The cacao nibs are raw, and the mint leaves are grown out back in the garden. They use oat milk ice cream. Drink it while you hold Handstand on the bar! Don't forget to tag me.

With wild eyes, I ripped off my shirt and screamed at the top of my lungs, "MINT CACAO CHIP SMOOTHIE HANDSTAND ON THE BAR!"

Carly and Asia came down from their Handstand and looked up. Misty paused in mid-selfie as the room went quiet. With a curious look on his face, Roge asked, "What did you say?"

"Mint Cacao Chip Handstand, NOW! ON THE BAR! Patrons of Cafe Thankful. Are you ready to feel sexy and spiritual as fuck?!"

The whole restaurant cheered and rose to their feet. I looked at Carly, Roge and Asia. "You, you, and you. Smoothie Handstand, NOW! On the bar! Mint Cacao Chip!"

Roge's mouth dropped open. "You are a fucking genius! I knew you were a Swami!" Roge turned to Misty, "Look out, Misty. Eddie may have just turned the corner."

Misty squealed, "No fair! I can't hold Handstand!"

Roge turned to the rest of us. "Carly, Asia, Ash, let's go!"

Misty yelled out, "Wait! Carly! Asia! Come back! Keep tagging me!"

Ashwala glared at Misty, "Your Boob Yoga is going down!"

Misty grabbed a fresh handful of alkaline ice cubes and rubbed them up and down her legs and on her chest. Her skin had a sheen from camera flashes as she returned to more erotic selfies.

Carly and Asia ran to the bar with their smoothies and right away flew up into a wicked Handstand. Roge wasn't far behind. He grabbed his drink and headed to the bar.

He turned back and said, "Come on, guys!" he waved to Ashwala and me. "Let's go! Quintuple Mint Cacao Chip Handstand on the bar! Oh man, Skone would have loved this one."

The image of Skone falling to his death flashed in front of my eyes. My mind cringed when I thought of Gordo and his smashed-in face, but I knew I had no choice. I grabbed my smoothie, stood up and was ready to make my way to the bar when Ashwala grabbed my arm.

"Eddie, wait. I can't do Handstand."

"It's okay. Wait here."

"No. See, I told Roge I could. That's why he offered me the job."

"What do you mean?"

"He said front-desk managers have to do Handstands on the desk every morning. I guess it's like some rule. They have to go Live and post a Handstand pic."

"You can't do Handstand!"

"I know I can't! I didn't have a choice. He promised me a job, and he said I'd be super spiritual. I thought I'd have time to practice. I didn't think he'd test me now!"

Guests gathered around the bar as Carly, Asia, and Roge were already upside down. "SEXY YOGIS! We have a new posture!" shouted Roge. "The first-ever Mint Cacao Chip Smoothie Handstand!"

The crowd grew as everyone pulled out their phones.

"I love it! Smoothie Handstand at Cafe Thankful feels so sexy!" glowed Asia, still upside down.

Carly added, "I feel so spiritual."

Lifting one hand off the bar, Roge held One-Handed Handstand and then grabbed his phone. He opened IG and posted a batch of selfies. "My Instagram is freaking going insane! Ten thousand likes! Five thousand new followers in sixty seconds." Roge yelled to the crowd, "Everyone, keep tagging SSAFY!"

Carly looked over and saw me still sitting with Ashwala. "Come *on,* guys, what are you waiting for?"

Roge shouted from the bar, "Bartender, throw some organic whip cream on top. Quintuple Handstand, baby!"

Asia yelled out, "Eddie! Ash! Come on! Misty's in the lead!"

"I guess it wouldn't hurt to try," said Ashwala in a desperate attempt to sound hopeful. "They do make it look easy."

The mental image of Skone's remains being scraped off the pier flashed before me, and then I saw the desperation in Ashwala's eyes.

"Ashwala, you don't have to do this. This is insane!"

"How 'bout I photobomb Misty's selfies!"

"Just wait here!"

I got up and slowly walked towards the counter. Roge came down from the bar and took some crowd selfies as people clapped and came up to pat him on the back.

Roge looked down at his phone."At last count, Misty is at 1,845,000 followers. Eddie, you're trailing a bit at 1-7-5 million."

I met Roge at the bar. "K, Roge. Ashwala is going to sit this one out."

"No-no-no. Ashwala, come on! Quintuple smoothie, here we go! We gotta introduce her to SSAFY Austin."

"How 'bout we do Quadruple Smoothie tonight. We'll test out the metrics. Test the filters, and if I win, then we do Quintuple tomorrow." I leaned in closer and whispered, "And Ashwala doesn't have a bikini or thong. We gotta get this one right."

Roge nodded and seemed more convinced. "Yeah, you're right. It'll look pretty silly if Ash isn't in a thong. We'll take her thong shopping tomorrow."

"Definitely, Roge."

"And I got a big new Euro thong sponsor coming through tonight. I'll premiere their booty floss tomorrow!"

Carly and Asia were still upside down on the bar.

"Come on, guys! Eddie, this feels amazing," shouted Carly.

Asia looked behind the counter. "Bartender, one more mint cacao chip smoothie for Sexy Eddie! Extra whip!"

Asia and Carly laughed. They pulled out their phones and held One-Handed Handstand while taking a sip from their smoothie. Meanwhile, Misty was still posing for the crowd, taking scratch and sniff selfies. She yowled, "I'm almost at 1.9 million followers! Swami, here I come!"

Ashwala leaped up from her chair and darted towards Misty.

"No. Ashwala, get away!" Ashwala started to make faces and photobomb Misty's selfies. Misty turned to Roge. "Roge! Ash and Eddie are cheating! She's photobombing me! *Roge!*"

Roge placed his phone on the bar in perfect IG Live position and hopped back onto the counter. I took a deep breath (my first in over six months) and slowly stepped up. When I looked to the crowd and saw the cell phones and flickering lights, I felt like the lead singer of a yoga pop band. Sweat dripped down my forehead. My heart started to beat faster. Like clockwork, the critical voices roared back again. *Eddie, you're going to flip over and kill yourself! You don't know how to do this! Get down! I have to do this. You're going to fall over and break your neck! You've never held Mint Cacao Chip Handstand before!*

Someone from the crowd yelled out, "Misty just hit 1.9! Eddie's trailing big time!"

Carly and Asia were sipping their smoothie in Handstand and taking video selfies when the bartender placed my drink down on the bar.

Carly could sense my apprehension. "You can do it, Eddie. Just like I showed you in class. It's all core. Engage the core."

I leaned over, pressed my hands firmly on the counter, and lifted one leg in the air. I took a few hops with my left leg but couldn't quite catch it.

"Just swing that other leg up in the air. Bartender, dim the lights. COME ON EVERYONE! LET'S HEAR IT FOR EDDIE!"

The lights turned down as more cheers rose from the crowd.

I inched my feet even closer to my hands and raised my hips in the air. I took a few more hops and carefully lifted my right leg up towards the ceiling. I tightened my core, brought my left knee into my chest, and was able to catch myself and float my torso in the air. The bartender turned on "Fly" by Sugar Ray as more people gathered and started to dance.

More cheers from the crowd. "Eddie! Eddie! Eddie!"

"You got this, Eddie! Lift the left leg!

Carly filled in: "Everybody, keep taking stories and tag us! You're about to witness the first-ever Quadruple Mint Cacao Chip Smoothie One-Handed Handstand!"

With my right leg in the air, I engaged my core and extended my left leg towards the ceiling. *AHHHH!!! I'm doing it! Smoothie Handstand with Roge, Carly, and Asia!*

Gordo's voice came back. *I'm so proud of you, Eddie. You're going to be the new Sexy Swami!*

The critical voices grew louder.

Don't fall over, you idiot! Tell Roge to take the selfie! Hurry! You're going to fall over! SSAFY is going to kill you, too! Get Down! NO! Take the selfie!

Asia yelled out, "GO, EDDIE! Take a sip of the smoothie! Roge, take the selfie!" Asia looked at the crowd. "KEEP TAGGING SSAFY!"

Asia lifted one hand off the bar, grabbed her phone, and took a few more group selfies as she held One-Handed Handstand.

"These are going to look so hot!"

Carly screamed at the top of her lungs, "I LOVE YOU, SSAFY! I FEEL SEXY AND SPIRITUAL AS FUCK!"

More applause and cheers from the crowd.

"Eddie's up to 1.8 million!"

Asia yelled, "Take a sip of the smoothie, Eddie!"

I looked over to Ashwala, who was still busy distracting Misty from her selfies. Ashwala looked up and saw me upside down on the bar. Her mouth dropped as I locked eyes with her.

"Come on, Eddie! You're so close!" someone shouted.

I looked down and opened my mouth, but the straw was too far away from my lips.

"You can do it! Just bend your elbows."

My entire body shook uncontrollably. "I'm going to fall."

Asia cried, "Roge, we're losing him."

Roge yelled, "Hang in there, Big-E! SSAFY is counting on you! Quadruple smoothie, baby!"

I managed to keep my balance as I pressed my legs higher in the air. I opened my mouth for one more try when my elbows started to violently shake.

"Asia! HELP!!!!!"

"EDDIE, NO!!!! Roge, take the selfie!"

My body completely gave out from underneath me.

CRASH BOOM BAM!!!!!

Everyone gasped with horror as the place went quiet.

Roge bellowed to the crowd. "What are you doing, people?! KEEP STORYING! TAG SSAFY! I will not let another fall go unstoried!"

As I fell, I hit the side of my head across the edge of the bar and landed flat on my back. I was knocked out cold. Blood trickled down the side of my head. Asia and Carly jumped down from their Smoothie Handstand and raced towards me.

Roge screamed out, "KEEP STORYING, PEOPLE! Do not stop the stories! Did any of you get that Live?"

A few people raised their hands.

"Tag SSAFY and DM that to me, now!"

Asia bent down next to me and brought her hands to my face.

"Wake up, Eddie! Roge! Is he okay?"

"He's a fucking yoga stud! His Instagram is going to go nuts! We did it, baby!"

"There's a lot of blood!"

"This is totally going viral. The more blood, the better."

Roge pressed his face against mine and took a few rounds of selfies.

Looking concerned, Asia asked, "Should we call 911?"

Roge was preoccupied with his selfies and replied, "Not yet, Asia. Just trying to find the right filter." Roge turned to the crowd. "Keep tagging SSAFY!"

In a flash, Misty emerged through the crowd and brought her Tata Yoga party to the floor next to me. She pressed her half-naked body against my face and took more selfies.

Roge pushed Misty away. "Misty, stop. I'm in a flow state."

Misty shoved back. "I have to be the Swami! Get away!"

Roge pushed again. "You're ruining my yoga high!"

Misty pressed her melons against my face and smiled to the camera. Snap-snap-snap. She turned and yelled to the crowd, "Keep tagging Mistyshower yoga!"

Someone screamed, "Misty's at 1-9-4!"

Roge pressed his loins against my face."Tag SSAFY!"

Misty yelled, "Mistyshoweryoga!"

Asia looked at her phone and found me on Instagram. "Guys! Eddie's gaining! He's at 1-9-2 million followers! It's gonna be a close one!"

Misty jumped on the bar and started to dance and twerk for the crowd. Roge got in a few more stories before setting my head back down on the ground. He stood up and shouted to the mob, "Everyone, he's going to be fine as long as you keep tagging SSAFY! If any of you want to take a selfie with Eddie before we get him to the hospital, one at a time, please!"

Ashwala pushed through the crowd and met Roge, who was staring down at his phone.

Ashwala yelled, "ROGE!"

Roge didn't hear her. He was focused on editing and cropping his pics.

She yelled again, "ROGE!"

Roge was still staring down at his phone. "Almost there…"

Ashwala shoved Roge in the chest.

"ROGE!"

"What?!"

"What are you doing!?"

"I'm taking selfies, what do you think I'm doing?!"

Ashwala bent down to check if I was breathing. She looked at Roge. "Did you call 911!?"

"Soon! Just hang on! This fall is going to be HUGE!"

Still dancing on the bar, Misty screamed, "I'm at 1-9-5!"

Carly yelled out, "Most spiritual day ever!"

Ashwala stood up and yelled, "All of you are insane! What is wrong with you people!?"

Roge replied, "What is wrong with you? Where is your phone, and why aren't you taking selfies?"

"We have to get him to a doctor!"

Roge replied, "And we will. Just as soon as I post this selfie."

"You are a pig, Roge. No yogi behaves this way!"

"Oh, please. This is yoga."

"This is not yoga!"

"Oh, and I heard about Sanctuary, Ash. It's over! SSAFY is king! I'm as yogi as they come, baby!"

"Yuck! Good-bye, Roge!"

"Maybe Vishy wants a job at SSAFY? He can teach about the yamas and the yabadabadoos and the diddley doos!"

Roge burst out laughing. Ashwala pushed Roge to the side and rammed her way through the crowd. She took out her phone and called 911.

A few minutes passed, and still no sign of an ambulance. Asia was rubbing my forehead with pH-balanced ice cubes and lavender oil, frantically trying to get me to snap out of it.

"Roge, he isn't waking up! We can't afford to lose another one."

As I lay sprawled out on the ground, Skyler managed to push her way through and make it up to the bar.

Asia looked up and yelled, "Skyler!"

Skyler replied, "What happened?!"

"Handstand crash."

"Which one?"

Carly answered, "Smoothie."

"Yikes. Has he done it before?"

"We worked on Green Juice yesterday," Asia said. "He looked like he was ready to go."

Roge shrugged his shoulders and said, "We had a little yoga contest to see who's going to be the Swami and then he kind of flipped over."

"Was it the Mint Cacao Chip?" Skyler asked.

Taking a sip of his smoothie, Roge answered, "Totally."

Skyler turned to the bartender. "One more Mint Cacao Chip smoothie. Make it to go!"

Roge took another gulp. "SSAFY is going to explode! Everyone is going to want to drink a smoothie AND hold a Handstand."

Carly added, "We'll workshop it next week!"

Skyler looked at her phone. "Roge. Your post. It's got 300,000 likes!" Skyler kept scrolling. "OH MY GOD!! Eddie just passed 1.95 million followers!"

Asia turned back to Carly. "Who shot the boomerang?!"

Carly yelled, "I did!"

Roge answered, "He's going to be Instafamous for sure."

"Where's the ambulance?" shouted Skyler.

Looking concerned, Asia answered, "Still not here! Eddie isn't moving! What do we do!?"

Carly grabbed her smoothie to go. "Roge, help me lift Eddie. We gotta scoot him to the SSAFY Emergency Room, now!"

Roge and Carly lifted me off the floor and lugged me through the crowd. The cheers, dancing, tags, selfies, and flashing lights moved towards the exit as we hurried out towards Rose Ave. With a look of worry, Misty could sense the crowd was getting ready to leave. "Wait! Where are you going?! I'm not at 2 million! Keep tagging me!" Misty frantically grabbed a glass from the bar and poured a Mint Cacao Chip smoothie over her body. "Don't go! Look! I have Mint Cacao Chip Smoothie all over me!"

Carly's Bird was parked on the sidewalk with a makeshift gurney on wheels attached to the back. Carly hopped on her Bird as Roge placed me down on the gurney.

"You're going to be okay, buddy. You're going to wake up and be the Swami. I can feel it. People are going to be doing Smoothie Yoga for years!"

Roge lay down next to me and took a few more selfies as Carly turned to face the crowd, "EVERYONE! LET'S GET EDDIE TO THE HOSPITAL! KEEP TAGGING SSAFY AND POSTING THOSE STORIES! GRAB A BIRD AND LET'S GO!!"

CHAPTER 14
A spiritual Awakening

"**H**is eyelids are moving!"

"Eeeeeddieeeeeee. Are you awwwwwaaaaakeeeeee?"

"You have over 2 million followerssssss. Wake uuuuppppp...."

"Look at what Rooooggggge is doing."

Asia leaned in and gave me a gentle kiss on the cheek.

"Eddie, we're so proud of you."

A white bandage was wrapped around my head. I was dizzy and nauseous. As I opened my eyes, I immediately felt a throbbing pain throughout my entire body. Roge was holding Strawberry Banana Smoothie Handstand while Carly was posting a Live video on Instagram.

"Hey, lovers. We're in the hospital with Eddie. We wanted to give you a little SSAFY update. He's breathing, and he should be waking up any second. He passed 2 million followers. Tagged in 675 posts, he's got 3,222 heart emojis, and my boomerang has 320,000 views! Great work, sexy yogis! Keep sending in those DMs, heart emojis, and keep posting your stories from last night.

All month we'll be highlighting the new Mint Cacao Chip Smoothie Handstand and why it's such a spiritual posture."

Asia lay down and leaned against me.

"Hi, baby. You okay for a few more selfies?"

"Sure."

"You reached 2 million followers!"

"I what?"

"You don't remember, do you?"

"Remember what?"

Carly put her phone down and took my hand.

"You held Mint Cacao Chip Smoothie Handstand with me, Roge, and Asia! You were incredible. Quadruple Smoothie Handstand. You're going to Austin as the new Sexy Swami. You'll be teaching Mint Cacao Chip Smoothie Handstand! Your classes are sold out!"

"Cafe Thankful is sponsoring you!" Asia filled in. "You never have to pay for a smoothie there again. The owner loves you. People want the Mint Cacao Chip Smoothie and try Handstand on the bar! Right where you flipped over!"

Misty jumped on the bed and hopped up and down. "We're going to Austin! I'm the front desk manager!" Roge came down from his Banana Berry Handstand. "Dude. You're famous. Never seen anything like it. You and Misty passed 2 million! You're both off to Austin! She's going to host daily Shower Yoga classes, and you're the Smoothie Yoga stud. We have sixty new smoothie sponsors. Cacao seeds, mint leaves, Shakeeta Bananas, Mary's Berries, alkaline ice cubes. Everyone wants to get on board!"

Asia gave me a hug. "We're so happy for you."

"I have the worst headache."

Asia put her hand against my forehead. "Your whole life is going to change. Roge is flying us to Thailand!"

Roge put his hand on my shoulder, "You, me, and Asia. Thailand. Smoothie workshops to teach yogis how to hold Smoothie Handstand. It's going to be sexy and spiritual as fuck!"

"But didn't I fall over?"

"Doesn't matter. Everyone wants to sip smoothies and do Handstand! I'm thinking we can go even bigger! Like Whip Cream or Honey Handstands. Cafe Thankful Handstand Yoga parties and smoothie workshops. You did it, man! We're going to be flying around the world teaching Smoothie Handstands, baby!"

"Then what am I doing in the hospital?"

Roge and the gang huddled up around me. Roge put his arm around my shoulder as Asia and Carly hopped on my bed and looked longingly into my eyes.

"Because SSAFY loves you, Big-E."

Carly added, "All those people outside want to be spiritual just like you."

"You want them to feel spiritual, too. Don't you?"

"Sure."

"And you love SSAFY, right?"

"Of course."

"I want to hear you say it, Big-E," Carly shoved her phone in my face. "Live on Insta to the whole SSAFY family."

"I... I love SSAFY."

"LOUDER!"

"I LOVE SSAFY!"

Roge put his face right up to mine and said, "And you want the whole world to be sexy and spiritual as fuck."

"Of course, Roge. I want everyone to be sexy and spiritual as fuck."

A sinister grin formed on Roge's face as he said, "Good, Sexy Swami."

Carly leaned over my bed. "Come on. One more group selfie, and let's get you out of here."

As Asia and Carly wheeled me out of the hospital, Roge held Handstand on the wheelchair handlebars and waved to the crowd. Nurses begged us for one last going-away group selfie. Hundreds of sexy yogis stood outside, celebrating the incarnation of Smoothie Yoga by drinking a Mint Cacao Chip Smoothie. I was a bona fide twenty-four-hour SSAFY yoga celebrity. A spiritual powerhouse. Everywhere I turned, sexy yogis asked for an autograph and congratulated me on becoming the new Sexy Swami.

Over the next few days, as I healed, Roge helped me pack my tank-tops, thongs, Speedos, and flip-flops. Giovanni, Leo, and Nellie became besties while Roge worked on his triple-cat ab selfies. Roge, Carly, and I had our first smoothie workshop in Thailand later in the week, and from there, we were off to Austin to celebrate the official grand opening of SSAFY Austin.

The plan was for Misty to watch Nellie and Leo and take hundreds of daily shower and cat selfies promoting SSAFY Austin before meeting me in Texas. It was Friday, the day before I was scheduled to leave for Thailand. Misty and I were on our way to

Whole Foods to collab with Roge and Asia. On the last Friday of each month, Roge scheduled SSAFY children's workshops in the produce aisle at local grocery stores. Roge liked to give back to the local community and used these workshops to teach kids how to take ab selfies while snacking on organic vegetables.

Misty and I parked our Birds and walked towards the entrance when I caught a glimpse of Ashwala sitting outside on a bench. Her head was down, and she was reading the latest issue of *Lion's Breath Weekly*. I was about to call out her name, but Misty turned my head and locked her arms around me. "One quick kissy-kissy selfie. My followers want to see us make out."

Misty yanked her phone out and with her lips pressed against mine, whispered, "I have a new lip balm sponsor. Kiss me harder, Big-E."

Just then, I heard my name being called out. Out of the corner of my eye, I saw Ashwala walking towards us.

Misty's lips were still planted on my face when I said, "Ashwala, hey!"

"I thought that was you!"

I tried to push away from Misty's tight grip.

Ashwala asked, "How's your head?"

"Little headache here and there, but I'll be fine."

Misty yelled out, "Posted it! Look at how spiritual we look!" Misty turned and noticed Ashwala standing next to me. "Oh, hi, Ash."

"Hey, Misty." Trying to be nice, she added, "Congrats on Austin."

"Super excited. No hard feelings?"

"Your Shower Yoga is going to go over great."

"Gosh, I hope so."

"Austin's perfect. The hot summers. Makes total sense."

Misty replied, "Wanna take a selfie with me and Eddie? Give your Insta a little bump?"

"I'm okay."

"Like a going away selfie. Maybe a belfie?"

"Kind of down on social media."

Misty's face scrunched up. "Eww. That's not very spiritual."

I turned to Misty. "Hey, why don't you go inside and take a few orange and carrot juice selfies. I'll be right in."

"Sure thing, baby. Don't miss me." Misty gave me another kiss, snapped a few more selfies, and marched inside.

Ashwala smiled and added, "You're... glowing!"

"Ha. Probably all the kissy-kissy selfies. Misty has a new sponsor. We have to take like 100 lip selfies a day."

"Wow. That's a lot of selfies."

"You get used to it. Hey, I haven't seen you since Thankful."

"Yeah, I meant to come see you at the hospital, but the entrance was blocked off by the paparazzi and all your fans."

"You should have texted me."

"It's okay. I saw Carly's Live stream. Not sure I really fit in with the SSAFY crowd."

"It's good to see you. You okay?"

"Hanging in there. Waiting tables at the Almond Nut until Vishy re-opens the studio." She sighed. "I heard you're going to Austin. I remember the first time you walked into Sanctuary."

"I was clueless."

"And now you're a Swami."

I smiled and added, "Sexy Swami."

There was an awkward silence before Ashwala blurted out, "I'll miss you."

"Yeah, we leave tomorrow for Thailand, then it's off to Austin."

"You're like yoga famous."

"I guess."

"You're in *Lion's Breath Weekly*, *Yoga Zen in the Den*, *Yoga Love Heart Kindly*. Every magazine is writing about how spiritual you are."

"You sure you don't want a quick selfie with a famous yogi?"

"You and selfies."

"Just one. I'm telling you. The selfies bring out the spirituality."

"I don't know."

"Trust me. You get all these emojis and DMs. People like you and follow you. Companies send you free clothes. You'll feel so spiritual."

"Okay, sure. Just one."

"Great! I'll hashtag #AlmondNut."

I leaned in next to Ashwala, wrapped my arm around her, and smiled to the camera. Just as I was about to take a selfie, I heard my name. Was it Skone? Gordo? Were the critical voices back again?

"Eddie, baby!"

Roge and Asia zipped into the parking lot on a new SSAFY certified scooter.

Roge parked and wailed, "Got a new sponsor, dude! You're going to love it! Look at this!" Roge ripped off his pants to reveal a thong with a selfie stick attached. "I can have a camera pointed right at my thong. Totally frees up my hands to take selfies, give some spanks or sign autographs. Twenty-Four Seven thong selfies or Live videos! Fucking genius. I just ordered you one!"

I looked at Ashwala, who was trying to keep from laughing.

Roge turned to Asia. "Show them!"

Asia took off her hoodie to reveal a bikini top attached to a selfie stick.

Roge looked at Ash. "Ash! That's all you! Bikini selfie stick! Twenty-four-hour eye or lip selfies. Whatever you want."

"I think I'm good, Roge."

"You sure? They're going to be HUGE!"

"I'll pass."

"K. Your loss. Eddie, you ready to teach these kids how to feel sexy and spirirtual as fuck?"

Roge turned to Ash. "You and me, little SSAFY hand massage later?"

Ashwala smiled, "Goodbye, Roge."

As Roge and Asia walked inside, I turned to Ashwala and gave her a hug.

"Good to see you, Ash."

"You, too." Ashwala smiled. "Say hi to Nellie and Leo for me."

"Say hi to Vishy."

Ashwala bowed her head towards me. "Namaste. May the light in me shine brighter in you."

I turned and looked around to make sure no one was looking and bowed my head.

"Namaste."

Ashwala's eyes widened. "Whoah, look at you. Saying Namaste. That's not very sexy."

"Roge would kill me."

"You're breathing much better."

"That's weird. I don't remember the last time I took a breath."

Ashwala smiled. "I'll tell Vishy you said hi."

"Hey, you should come to Austin. Take my class."

"I'll think about it."

Ashwala waved goodbye and walked away. I turned to meet the rest of the SSAFY crew when all of a sudden, my chest grew tight. I felt light-headed, and the negative voices came roaring back. *Did you just say Namaste? What the fuck is wrong with you? Did you bow your head AND say Namaste?! Roge would kill you! I was trying to be nice. Ash is my friend. She still talks about the breath! She said Namaste! None of that is yoga! Do I STILL have to remind you yoga has nothing to do with breathing or saying Namaste?! Okay! I got it! Get inside and teach those kids how to take ab selfies, NOW! Take Cucumber Handstand with Roge! You have to take more lip selfies with Misty. You have a new cacao seed sponsor. You owe them a cacao seed selfie, and don't forget to tag them! AND you have to go home and take cat selfies with Nellie and Leo! You're the Swami, Eddie! The world is counting on you. Get in there and teach those kids how to feel sexy and spiritual as fuck!*

I'm thankful for the voices. The way they keep me focused on the important aspects of yoga. Whether it's Gordo, Skone, Roge, or my own critical voice, they're always with me. Reminding me to focus on my phone, pay more attention to Instagram, work on my abs and do what I can to help the world feel sexy and spiritual. I hope Ashwala flies out to see me. I could show her around the city and we could take hundreds of selfies. Bridge and smoothie selfies. A green juice kayak selfie. Maybe a Speedo Barton Springs selfie. Definitely a triple cat ab selfie. Me, Nellie, Leo, and Ash. Now that would be spiritual as fuck.

The SSAFY Goodie-Bag

Congratulations, sexy yogis. You're one step closer to experiencing the greatest yoga highs of your life. Remember, as long as your awareness is on your abs, your buttocks, and making your Instagram look sexy AF, you'll be on your way to a sexier and more spiritual YOU!

When you join SSAFY, you'll receive an SSAFY goodie-bag filled with elixirs, tanning oil, a bathing suit, selfie stick, moisturizer, and a bottle of green juice. You'll get pamphlets, brochures, and exercises to help you jump-start your SSAFY lifestyle. These brochures serve as a how-to guide on the Selfie Standing Postures, lifestyle tips, the SSAFY sexy limbs of yoga, how to use Instagram to pick a sexy yoga instructor, and even SSAFY philosophy. While the most spiritual way to experience SSAFY is in person, I wanted to include a few items from my goodie-bag to help you kick off your SSAFY yoga journey. For those of you who don't live in LA or Austin, be sure to follow your favorite SSAFY teacher on IG and subscribe to the SSAFY YouTube channel.

Picking A Sexy Yoga Teacher

Finding a sexy yoga teacher will be one of the most important decisions you will make in your practice. For those of you who live near one of the SSAFY studios, it's a no-brainer. Roge, Carly, Asia, Skyler, Jo, or Misty will be a logical choice. But what do you do if you don't live near SSAFY Austin or Los Angeles? There are over 455,000 yoga teachers in the United States, so how do you know which teacher is right for you? How do you find that special teacher who will inspire you to take ab selfies #everydamnday?

Thanks to Instagram, it's never been easier to find a yoga teacher who will entice you to step onto your mat. Type in the words "sexy yoga teacher" in the IG search, and instantly, thousands of yoga teachers will appear in your search. Scroll through the different profiles and zero in on what inspires you the most. Maybe you want a teacher with tattoos and piercings. Do you want a teacher with hot abs like Gordo? Maybe you're inspired by a teacher with a tight ass? You could even add a few

keywords to help narrow down your search: huge _______ long
_______ thick _______ erotic_______ (you fill in the blank).

Once you find a teacher who meets your spiritual desires, go
ahead and send them a DM. Tell them you're on the hunt for a
new yoga teacher and you're interested in taking one of their
classes. Set up an IG chat session so you can ask questions about
their teaching style. Do they spank a lot in class? What kind of
music do they like to play? Do they take a lot of stories and tag
students in class? What do they typically wear when they teach?
Do they give a lot of hands-on or body-to-body adjustments?
Would they feel comfortable rubbing massage oil over your body
during class? What about post-class group selfies for IG? And
when you're done talking with them, do you feel spiritually
aroused? Do you feel inspired to work on your abs and take more
selfies? With Instagram, your sexy yoga teacher is just a quick
search, click, and DM away.

The Selfie Standing Postures

With hundreds of different yoga postures to choose from, you
can trust that SSAFY knows which poses are proven to create the
most spirituality inside your body. After the conference in Vegas,
Asia and Carly went back to their home studio and performed
an SSAFY/IG spiritual experiment. They examined every yoga
posture from Forward Folds, Back Bends, Restorative Poses,
Twists, Inversions, Standing Postures to even boring postures
like Savasana. They realized the only way they could accurately
measure each posture's level of spirituality was to post a selfie
in each pose. For consistency, they wore the same bikini and

sunglasses, used the same IG filter, and held each posture in the exact same spot on the Vegas Strip. From there, they tabulated the total number of likes, followers, and heart emojis and created a sexy yoga algorithm to determine each posture's level of spirituality. By the end of their research, it was clear which poses were the most spiritual and should be the focus of SSAFY and which postures should be dropped altogether.

Postures like Child's Pose, Happy Baby, and Savasana scored low with very few likes, comments, and heart emojis. With such a sub-par score in their algorithm, these poses were eliminated immediately. Postures such as Handstand, Crow Pose, and Scorpion scored very high with record numbers of likes, emojis, comments, and new followers. These postures were kept and remain the primary focus at most SSAFY classes, but Asia and Carly went a step further in their research. Even though postures like Warrior One didn't score as high, they're still included because they build up the strength needed to eventually hold some of the more spiritual and strenuous postures like Handstand.

While postures like Handstand and Crow will undoubtedly make you feel more spiritual, the Selfie Standing Postures are great "building blocks." They will strengthen your core and give you the confidence needed to master some of the more challenging postures at SSAFY. Take your time with these postures and have fun with them. Try them at the beach, on top of your car, or maybe in the park wearing a sexy bathing suit. And remember, don't forget to tag SSAFY!

Warrior One Selfie Pose

- Strengthens your shoulders, arms, legs, ankles, and back

- Opens your hips, chest, and lungs

- The arms are directly in front of the face in perfect selfie alignment

- Carly's spanks feel super spiritual in this posture

- Like count average: 5,800

- Heart emoji average: 1,125

- New follower average: 875

Warrior Two Selfie Pose

- Stretches your hips, groins, and shoulders

- Opens the chest and lungs

- Stimulates the abdominal organs

- An ideal standing posture while watching Hulu or Netflix

- Average like count: 8,400

- Heart emoji average: 2,076

- New follower average: 1,175

- Favorite variation on IG: Double Selfie Warrior Two

Double Selfie Warrior Two Pose

- Great for building strength in the biceps and triceps

- Ideal for your panoramic 360-degree selfies

- Average like count: 10,320

- Currently averages more emojis than any other Standing Posture

- Ranks as the most spiritual Standing Posture at SSAFY when you get double spanked by Asia and Carly

Triangle Selfie Pose

- Strengthens knees, ankles, abdominals, obliques, and back
- Relieves stress around the neck and lower back
- Average like count: 10,200
- Heart emoji average: 2,300
- New follower average: 2,050
- Suggested variations:
    - Out to brunch
    - On a moving escalator
    - At a drive-in movie theater
    - Watching the sunset
    - On top of your roof

Crescent Moon Selfie Pose

- Stretches the legs, groins, and hip flexors
- Strengthens and tones the thighs, hips, and booty
- Phone is perfectly aligned for selfies
- Average like count: 14,400
- Suggested variations:
    - Shower Crescent
    - Full Moon Crescent
    - Grocery Store Crescent
    - Dog Park Crescent

Side Angle Selfie Pose

- Relieves stiffness in the shoulders and back while providing a deep stretch to the groins and hamstrings. Strengthens the legs, knees, abdominal muscles

- The upper arm is stretched overhead in ideal selfie position

- Average like count: 17,650

- Suggested variations:
    - Movie Theater Side Angle
    - Football and Baseball Game Side Angle
    - Pet Your Dog Side Angle
    - Pedicure and Manicure Side Angle

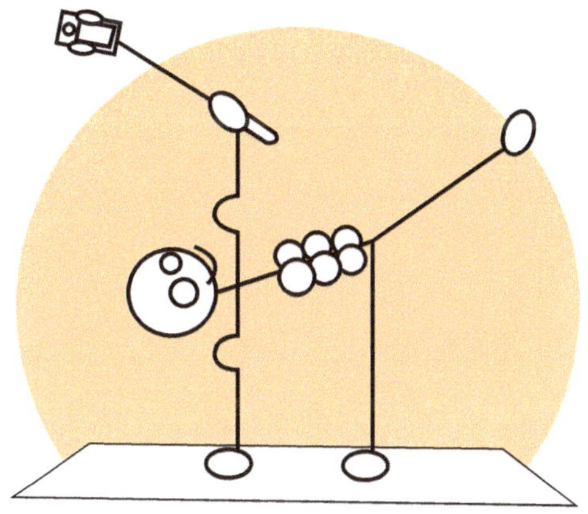

Selfie Half Moon Pose

- Strengthens the abdomen, ankles, thighs, buttocks, and spine
- Stretches the groins, hamstrings and calves, shoulders, chest, and spine
- Improves coordination and sense of balance
- Selfies from above, below, left, and right
- Consider attaching a camera to your foot for wide-angle selfies
- Average like count: 21,100
- Average emoji count: 8,762

SSAFY *Mantras*

"When you meet someone for the first time, ask them how many followers they have. That way, you know if it's worth being their friend."

"I start each day by posting a selfie of my ass. If it gets over 1,000 likes, then I know it's going to be a spiritual day."

"I had no time for selfies and Instagram today, so today actually never happened."

"Instagram is in early negotiations with the universe to add a 25th hour. The goal is to give users an extra hour to take more selfies."

"I'm only friends with people who have a good ass."

"If you don't have a six-pack, you suck at yoga."

"You're not truly living unless you've taken off all your clothes on Instagram."

"The SSAFY optometry office is now performing new eye filter implant surgery which involves putting the Instagram filters directly into your eyes. Now everyone can look sexy even when you're not using Instagram."

"If you can't 'like' my post within an hour, don't even bother. You're too late."

epilogue

I will never forget the first time I stepped into a yoga class. I could barely walk or move my wrists and arms. My body was wracked with excruciating pain. I was popping over ten pills a day, and I had a fever of 102. I was anemic. I lost over forty pounds. I was gaunt, and on top of the physical issues, I was riddled with anxiety. I was diagnosed with Rheumatoid Arthritis when I was twelve years old, and while the disease had been in remission for almost five years, when I turned twenty-four, the disease came back with a vengeance. It was one of the darkest periods of my life until one day, my therapist suggested I should try an Iyengar yoga class. I didn't know a thing about yoga, but I was desperate to feel better and figured I had nothing to lose. I started going to class four times a week, and over the next few years, I was able to come off all of my medication. I felt stronger, more confident and less anxious, and I am proud to say I have been in remission and off all of my medication for over twenty years.

When I started practicing yoga, there was no such thing as Instagram or Facebook. My teacher didn't use Instagram or take selfies or share "stories" to bring attention to herself or her practice. She didn't take side-angle booty shots or hold postures in a bikini. She didn't try to "inspire" her followers on a social media platform. She didn't have to curate her life in a particular way or try to create a "brand." My teacher's primary focus was to help me feel better. My practice was raw and ugly. It was personal, challenging, and lethargic, but for me, it was a matter of life and death. There was nothing fancy. No Handstands or upside-down show-off postures. Just yoga. It changed my life, and that's what's so powerful about the practice when it's in good hands. Yoga has the ability to heal and transform people's lives. It certainly changed mine, and it's why years later, I felt inspired to become a yoga teacher.

When Instagram became popular, I began to see its side effects trickle down into the yoga community. The "best" yoga teachers weren't the ones with the most teaching experience or the ones with the most knowledge, or the ones with the most depth. The most popular "teachers" were the ones who looked the sexiest or could hold wild variations of extreme postures like Handstand. They had a keen ability to market themselves and grab people's attention. Yoga was falling victim to the downward trend in our culture. Less depth and more superficiality. Less quiet and more noise. Less subtlety and more force.

Tristan Harris is an American technology ethicist. He is the president and co-founder of The Center for Humane Technology and he writes that tech and social media have created a "human downgrade" in our culture. If more people are becoming addicted to the allure and quick fix of technology and social media, then what is the effect on our society? What happens to human beings' innate need for connection if these devices, we rely so heavily on, are actually creating more passive behavior and disconnection. I became a yoga teacher because I wanted to remind students the value and immense "upgrade" that comes from turning off the phone, listening to the breath, being more present and living a life with less distractions. Of course I can see the convenience of technology but have we reached the tipping point where tech and social media are actually creating more harm than good.

Maybe Instagram, Facebook, and social media are simply the result of living in a capitalist world where money is the driving force. Maybe human beings, by nature, are insecure and crave constant validation and attention. Maybe the vast majority of people would prefer to just numb out, scroll and stare at Netflix or Instagram all day.

When was the last time you truly listened to the sound of your own breath? When's the last time you had a face-to-face conversation with someone and you truly listened? Can you go an hour without staring at a screen? Are you just waiting for this book to be finished so you can get back to your phone? I sure hope not, unless, of course, you want to take a selfie of your butt cheeks. Then go for it. Your followers will love it. You may even get a few sponsors. Maybe a thong sponsor. Maybe even a few hundred new followers. Oh, and don't forget to tag me. That would be sexy and spiritual AF.

Namaste

I'm not sure how I imagined that I was remotely qualified or had the mental stamina to sit down and write a book. This was by far the most painstaking, gut wrenching, yet creatively satisfying endeavor I've ever embarked on. It's one thing to write a three or four minute song, to produce a podcast, teach a yoga class or DJ a night club. But to try and put 50,000 words collectively on "paper" and somehow create a story that resonates or makes one iota of sense, is beyond anything I could have done by myself. I mean sure, it's my name on the cover and I may have been the one punching the keyboard, but this was a team effort. Considering I spent most of my time staring at a computer screen with no idea what the hell I was doing, I owe an enormous amount of gratitude to a select group of people who encouraged me through the tunnel and shoved me through to the other side.

To Dr. Rudin who had the sense I should try taking a yoga class and introduced me to my first yoga teacher. To Beth for being a true gem of a human being and for changing my life forever. You're a real yoga teacher. To Tamal and Sesa for tolerating my bad jokes in teacher training and for resisting the cultural trend towards more flash and staying true to who you are. To Jen, Tony, Danielle, Emily, Dinna, Ethan, Sienna, Diana, Brad, Joey, Warren and Dana for being the "first readers" of my putrid first draft and combatting the temptation to tell me to throw it away and give up. Somehow you made me feel like I should keep going.

To my Mom for reading, editing, reading, editing, more reading and editing and putting your Masters in English to good use. You could have made a killing as a literary editor. To my Dad for passing down his work ethic. I know you didn't have any idea what the heck I was doing, but you had a sense it was all going to be worth it in the end. To Aaron for being one of the most encouraging and supportive people I have ever been lucky to meet. Whether it's my music, our phone calls, or in this case, my book, your support and kind words stay with me days after you speak them. To Kristen for creating the imagery for this story and for understanding the crazy world living inside of my head. To Clint and Sofia for being consummate pros and creating the visual and verbal SSAFY world better than I could have ever imagined.

To Rony, behind the sunglasses and fancy cars, you are one of the most sensitive, heartfelt human beings I have met. Thanks for the constant encouragement and for reminding me there are good people left in the world. To Bruce, Kevin, Jake, Dan, Tim and Phil for making the last two years of my life such a joy as you helped me create a record while I was busy writing this book. To all of my podcast guests who remind me the power of good conversation and the value of truly listening. Emmy, you fill my heart with love #everydamnday and give me the constant support and freedom to pursue my creative passion projects. Whether I'm podcasting, singing, writing music or slouched over in front of a computer screen way past my bedtime, your love is undeniable. To Leo and Nellie for being the best cats in the world.

About the Author

Eddie is a musician, singer, songwriter, and producer who has produced and recorded four studio albums. *If I'm Happy It Ends, Stay With Me, Guarantee Me Love* and his latest record, *Dystopian Days*, are available on all streaming services or for purchase at eddiecohn.bandcamp.com. Eddie is the producer, host and creator of the podcast, *The Downward Facing Spiritual Spiral*, where he discusses with fellow artists, writers, and yoga teachers, the effects of technology and social media on the world as well as the creative landscape. Past guests have included Geographer, Aaron Byrd, Matt Dery, Joseph Arthur, Joanne Gerstner, Jen Wiederstrom, and Jimmy Gnecco. Eddie is a certified yoga instructor currently teaching private and in-studio public yoga classes, and he can also be found DJing in clubs around the city of Los Angeles. If you couldn't tell by now, Eddie also loves cats. Be sure to follow Eddie on all social sites @eddiecohn or visit ssafyoga.com or iameddiecohn.com.